P

Q

"Look at them all," said Ruth, rearing up in her seat to stare along the body of the plane, "eating pre-packed food on the way to Paris! What's the matter with them? They have no style."

"We have style," I said.

"We have style with a dash of panáche," said Ruth.

"Dashing but not flashy," I said.

"Not flash and not rash," said Ruth.

"Oh, I like to think we're rash," I said. "Yes, we're definitely rash. We're the wild women dropping out of the skies onto Paris just because we feel like it."

"Your spirits have certainly gone up," said Ruth.

"Right up," I said. "My spirits and I are about three thousand feet up."

"My spirits and I are with you," said Ruth, "and ready to handle any problems we may meet."

"We won't meet any problems," I said. "I hereby declare Paris a problem-free zone."

Unfortunately, Paris didn't seem to understand that.

Judy Allen has written over 30 published titles. She has won the Earthworm Award, the Whitbread Children's Novel Award and been Commended for the Carnegie Medal.

Paris
Quest

Judy Allen

RED FOX

A Red Fox Book

Published by Random House Children's Books
20 Vauxhall Bridge Road, London SW1V 2SA

A division of Random House UK Ltd
London Melbourne Sydney Auckland
Johannesburg and agencies throughout the world

1 3 5 7 9 10 8 6 4 2

First published simultaneously in
hardback and paperback by
Julia MacRae and Red Fox 1996

Phototypeset by Intype, London
Printed and bound in Great Britain by
Cox & Wyman Ltd, Reading, Berkshire

RANDOM HOUSE UK Limited Reg. No. 954009

Papers used by Random House UK Limited
are natural, recyclable products made from wood
grown in sustainable forests. The manufacturing
processes conform to the environmental regulations
of the country of origin.

ISBN 0 09 943701 5

For Laura

CONTENTS

1	The Girl with the Silver Case	1
2	A Wild Woman Makes a Decision	10
3	The First Six Problems	15
4	The Dogsbody Takes Flight	24
5	The Right People are not in Town	34
6	The Power Women	41
7	The Essential Paris	47
8	The Best Place	55
9	Doubts and Fears	65
10	The Heavy in the Lobby	76
11	Entering Without Breaking	87
12	And the Number You Need is . . .	94
13	The Site in Question	103
14	Out of the Depths	115
15	An Unusual Angle	123

CHAPTER ONE

The Girl with the Silver Case

If I'd known what was going to happen I'd have worn different clothes.

Possibly my best ones.

But my stars for the week had said – "Now is the time to consolidate your position and impress others with your practical skills" – which didn't sound like anything worth dressing up for.

I was standing in the Quest Travel shop, tidying up the brochure racks. This job was very slightly more interesting than standing in the Quest Tours office, doing the filing, but only very slightly.

I did want to get into the travel business, eventually, but I never meant to work for my parents. It's such a small outfit that everyone does long hours and Mum and Bill are the only ones who seem to get to go anywhere. Even Dad says he doesn't know why he bothers to keep his passport up to date.

Mum runs Quest Tours – Planned Package Holidays for People who are Seeking Something (antiques, ghosts, steam railways, UFOs, rare carnivorous beetles, the usual things). She and Bill do most of the foreign trips, fixing deals with hotels and stuff.

Dad runs Quest Travel which is the Travel Agency part of the operation. Quest Travel sells Quest Tours, but it also sells all kinds of other package deals as well. We have all the big names here. I should know. Half my time is spent gathering up their great heavy shiny slithery brochures and putting them back into the right places.

I had great plans for my year off, between school and college. I decided I was going to get casual work. I was only going to pick jobs that were interesting and very well paid. Then, when I had my dosh piled up, I was going to travel the world with my friend Ruth.

But I couldn't get a job. It wasn't just that I couldn't get an interesting job, or that I couldn't get a well-paid job – it was that I couldn't get any kind of job.

So when the Joint Managers of Quest Tours and Travel came down to breakfast one day, cracked open a new pack of Shredded Wheat, and said they could do with some help around the office, it was an offer I couldn't refuse.

My job title? I'm not sure. Up till that afternoon you could have called me a Girl Friday who works Monday through Saturday. You could have called me a Dogsbody, a Slave, an Underling, a Menial Minion. You could have called me Fed Up.

Peggy was behind the counter, trying to sort out a thin woman in a raincoat who seemed to think she could get from Turkey to Bolivia by rail. Mum and Bill were in the upstairs office, planning a Quest for

Antiques Tour. Dad was in the back office doing phone bookings. Mick doesn't come in on Tuesdays. So there wasn't even anyone to talk to.

The street door crashed open and someone tall lurched in backwards followed by three Munchkins – two of them shouting at each other and the third shouting at both of them to shut up.

I knew the tall one was Ruth. I'd recognise her hair anywhere – red and wild, with silver and turquoise Navajo beads threaded on the bit that hangs down the middle of the back. She says she doesn't have to lose her American identity just because she lives in England. Not that her ancestors are Navajo – mostly Irish, I think.

Ruth revolved slowly until she was facing me, and I could see she was carrying too many shopping bags to have come in frontwards. She put the bags down and watched them fall slowly over onto their sides. Two tins of pilchard and kidney cat food rolled out of one of them. "I'm living in a nightmare!" said Ruth.

The biggest of the three Munchkins, who I could now see was her half-brother George, detached himself from the others and came straight up to me. "Hi Jo," he said. "Will you buy a raffle ticket to Save the Whales?"

"Certainly," I said. "Apart from anything else, this is the most exciting thing that's likely to happen today."

"You sound as happy as I feel," said Ruth, catching up with the cat food and trying to prop the bags up against each other.

The thin woman in the raincoat had looked round

and frowned at the noisy intrusion. Now she turned back to Peggy, who seemed to have about forty-five brochures, charts and timetables on the counter in front of her. Peggy is even older than Mum and she never gets impatient. She just nodded calmly as the woman yacked on at her, and then hit the keys and began to call up some more information on the computer.

"Well *look* at me," I hissed at Ruth. "I stand in here watching people who don't deserve it planning to go off all over the world and I don't get to travel any further than Gareth does stacking his super-market shelves."

"Not as far, probably," said Ruth. "He goes up and down miles of aisles. According to you, you just go from one shelf to another. And back again."

"Thank you. That really cheers me up."

"I'd swap any day," said Ruth. "I've got those." She pointed to the two remaining Munchkins who were struggling on the floor in desperate battle, look-ing like some kind of semi-humanoid spider.

"What *are* those?" I said. "I've never seen them before."

"I only got them today," said Ruth, "after I lost my job at the dry-cleaners."

"What went wrong?"

"They closed down."

"You didn't tell me!"

"It was real sudden. So now I get paid to stop these two killing each other while their mother is doing more interesting things. I keep an eye on George, too, but I don't mind that. I like George."

George flapped his book of raffle tickets at me. I

got my bag out from behind the counter and shook it so I could locate the money by the sound. There was a chinking noise in the bottom left hand corner. I reached through several miniature bottles and jars, numerous peppermints (some still in their wrappings), a spare hairclip, six packs of airline sugar Bill had given me – big deal – and some partly shredded paper hankies, and found him a couple of coins.

"What do I win?" I asked.

"A week in Tunisia, or a mountain bike, or a personal stereo," said George, "if you get first, second or third. Otherwise it's just gift vouchers, but those won't be any good to you."

Ruth bent over the struggling mass and separated it into its two halves. The halves glared at each other and tried to kick.

"Wouldn't it have been better just to take one of them?" I said. "You know, divide and conquer?"

"They come as a set," said Ruth. "They live next door. One's a bully and the other whines – but I can never remember which is which."

"Here," said George, handing me my ticket. "Hope you win."

"Why won't the gift vouchers be any good?" I asked, remembering what he'd said.

"Because you'd lose them."

I took a swipe at his head with a fistful of promotional leaflets, but he'd just bent down to write my address on the ticket stub and I missed.

The twins lost interest in each other and caught sight of the bottom rack of brochures. I knew exactly what would happen. It was what always happened with anyone under six. They saw bright colours, they expected pictures, they dragged out a brochure, they spent ten nano-seconds staring at photographs of hotel swimming pools, they got bored, they ditched the brochure, and they dragged out the next one. They wouldn't stop until everything that had been on the bottom shelf was on the floor. Then they'd start on the next shelf up.

"I've just tidied that lot," I said. I knew I sounded like someone's nagging mother, but I couldn't help it.

"Sorry," said Ruth. "I brought them in here because I thought it was one place they couldn't do any damage. Also I thought it'd be nice to be somewhere where there wasn't any candy they could ask for."

I said, "Don't worry – I haven't got anything better to do."

Ruth said, "We sound like two old women grumbling at a bus stop."

"We might as well be!" I said. "When I think how envious everyone was when they heard I'd be working here! I bet they thought I'd be travelling all over the world. I bet they thought Dad would say 'pick a destination – any destination – the world is your oyster.' But he didn't, and he won't, and it isn't. It's ironic, really."

"You want irony?" said Ruth. "My godmother says I can use her airmiles, but I can't fly anywhere because I haven't got enough money to stop-over when I get there."

I thought about Ruth's godmother, who travels all over the world selling computer software, and I imagined how many airmiles she must have earned.

"You're right, the world isn't your oyster, either,"

I said. "It's such a stupid expression anyway – how could the world be an oyster?"

"Oh I don't know," said Ruth. "What *is* an oyster? An expensive and occasionally poisonous shellfish that's extremely difficult to get into. Yup, that sounds like the world as I know it."

I heard Bill come clattering down the stairs at high speed, the way he always does. Then he strode in and went straight to the shelves at the back and started to rustle his way through stuff, looking for a phone number or something I suppose.

I'm sure they've got all the numbers they could possibly need upstairs. I'm sure he only comes down as often as he does because he gets bored and wants to see what's going on.

I wouldn't admit it, even to Ruth, but I used to think a lot about what I was going to wear each day because of Bill. I gave up after three weeks when I found he never looked at me. I mean he literally never looked at me. He would talk to me, sometimes, but he was always looking at whatever bit of paper he was working with – or at the customers – or out of the door in case anyone interesting was going by.

In fact you could say it was Bill's fault I wasn't looking my best that Monday.

He's quite old, he's more than thirty, and I don't know that I even like him very much, but there *is* something about him. There must be, or I wouldn't spend so much time thinking how annoying he is.

He's tall. He's fit – plays squash, swims, all that stuff. He's got dark hair and very dark eyes and I've heard a rumour that he has a way of looking at you that can turn you into melting jelly. I wouldn't know, since he never looks at me in any way at all, but I have seen him make a bad-tempered, unreasonable customer into a nice human being. Only if it's a female customer, naturally.

Ruth watched Bill as he swung into sight and started flapping things about on the back shelf. Then she grabbed my arm and pulled me round the other side of her so she could whisper with her back to him. "*That* must cheer up the working day," she muttered.

He can't have heard what she said, but the mumbling sound got his attention, and he looked over at her – definitely *at* her, not through her or past her. He picked up what he'd been looking for, waved it triumphantly over his head, and grinned at Ruth. He has a lopsided grin. I swear he practises it in front of a mirror.

"Hi, can we help?" he said.

"I'm a friend of Jo's," said Ruth. "Just passing through."

"Pass through any time," said Bill, focusing very carefully on her red hair, her blue eyes, and then the rest of her. "Why didn't you tell me you had such a beautiful friend, Jo?"

"It must have slipped my mind," I said, trying not to clench my teeth. "This is Ruth. Ruth, that's Bill."

"At school together, were you?" said Bill, still looking at Ruth.

"S'right," said Ruth.

"Well, Ruth," said Bill, striding out of the doorway towards the stairs and then sticking his head back in again, "when you grow up you're going to be quite something." He vanished.

"That puts me in my place," said Ruth.

"He is *so* patronising," I said, giving up the effort not to clench my teeth.

"He's got a cute smile, though," said Ruth. "Kind of lopsided."

"I think it makes him look as though he's got toothache," I said.

"No you don't," said Ruth.

"No, I suppose I don't," I said crossly.

The street door opened and a girl of about our own age – 17 going on 18 – staggered in. She was blonde and annoyingly pretty and her jeans fitted her just right and she had on the very pair of short boots I'd have bought at the weekend if I could have afforded them. She was staggering because she was carrying a large, square, silver-coloured case that was obviously very heavy. She looked desperate.

She put the case down in the middle of the floor and stared blankly at me and Ruth and George and the kids. She looked at her watch, moaned, picked up the case again and went to queue behind the woman in the raincoat, hopping from foot to foot and biting her thumb nail.

Bill, I thought, you left the room too soon. Hard luck.

I walked quickly round behind the other end of the counter, where I wouldn't crowd Peggy's space, and called out, "Good morning, can I help you?"

And that was really the start of it all.

CHAPTER TWO

A Wild Woman Makes a Decision

The girl had put the case down again, but as soon as she realised I wasn't just another customer, she picked it up and rushed across to me so fast I thought she'd collide with the counter.

I braced myself.

It wasn't just that I wanted to impress Ruth and George – I really thought there was the faint possibility she might ask a question I could answer. And if not I had instructions to grab Dad between calls and get him out to the counter.

"Oh, I do hope you can help," the girl was saying, even before she reached me. "I've made the most awful muddle and I'm just hoping you can sort it out because otherwise I don't know what's going to happen except that I should think I'll lose my job."

She heaved the case up, thudded it onto the counter right in front of me, and began to open it.

Ruth said afterwards it had looked as if she was going to try and sell me something.

George said he'd thought she was going to pull a gun on me and demand all the foreign currency and a ticket to South America.

I don't remember what I thought, but I do remember I stepped backwards quite quickly.

When she had the lid open, though, I could see it was a fitted camera case, with bits of camera, lenses, filters, film, all tucked into specially-shaped compartments.

"What's the problem?" I said rather feebly. I was confused, but I was beginning to feel sorry for her.

"My boss has gone to Paris without this," she said. "I can't believe it's happened, it's so awful – we booked through Quest Travel – we always book through you – several times a year – but not always Paris of course – my boss is called Clair Aitken – I expect you can look it up if you need to check – and there are two or three camera boxes in the studio – and it's my job to pack them – and this is the one with the best camera-body and all the right lenses – and the film's in here too – though it's easy to get more 35 mil film – but it's the lenses that really matter – and Clair picked up the wrong box – and I didn't notice – I should have checked – I should have kept them quite separate – and now it may be too late – the plane went ages ago – and Clair's going to be out there without the right stuff and it's all my fault and I shall get into trouble – and I expect I'll be fired . . ."

I was quite glad when she ran out of breath because my head was spinning.

Then a strange thing happened. My head seemed to spin all the way down to my heart. My heart started thumping. The thumping worked its way up to my throat and my voice began to speak all by itself. Instead of asking her to wait till Peggy was free, instead of going through the back and asking Dad how we were supposed to handle all this, instead of doing anything sensible, I stood right where I was and smiled at her. And my voice said, "Don't worry, leave it to us, we'll get it out there today. Just give me the details."

The words had a dramatic effect on everyone who heard them, including me.

The girl half collapsed onto the counter in relief and began to say, "Oh thank you, oh that's marvellous, oh I'm so grateful," over and over again.

Ruth and George moved close in behind her and stared at me in amazement.

And me? I panicked. But it was too late for that. There was no way out, not with all that gratitude splashing about the place.

My voice, having said its bit, switched itself off again, and I handed her a pad and pencil without a word. She grabbed it and began to write things down – Clair Aitken, the name and address of a hotel, things like that.

Then she did a bit more of the gratitude stuff and left – though not before George, seeing his chance, offered her a raffle ticket. She was in such a great mood, she bought the rest of the book.

Ruth came up and leant on the counter, admiring the open camera box. "You were cool," she said, as I closed the lid and snapped the clips shut.

My voice came back under my control. "You have to look as if you know what you're doing," I said, managing to sound as calm as Peggy. "Otherwise everything falls apart."

"So how do you get it out there?" said Ruth. "You call a courier service, right?"

"No," I said, "I'm going to take it myself."

Ruth's eyes opened wide. "Is that what your parents would expect you to do?"

"I shouldn't think so," I said.

Ruth narrowed her eyes to tiny slits. "You're not supposed to make those kind of decisions, are you?" she said. "You're supposed to fetch someone else, am I right?"

Ruth knows me too well.

"Everyone else is busy," I said reasonably.

"I bet Bill would've come down and helped," said Ruth, grinning (but not lopsidedly).

"I *could* have asked Bill to come back in and patronise me," I said with dignity, "if that's what I'd wanted. But I decided to use my initiative instead. I'm here to run errands, aren't I?"

Ruth was seriously impressed. She didn't even try to hide it. "You're a wild woman!" she said.

"I am," I said, "I'm wild with boredom! But I can be tamed if I can have fresh French fries genuinely fast-fried in France for lunch."

"As a true friend," said Ruth, "I'm trying hard not to be jealous – but it ain't easy!"

"Come with me," I said.

Ruth stared at me.

"I don't want to go alone," I said, suddenly realising how true that was.

Ruth still didn't answer.

"Come *on*," I said. "You can't say no! All we have to do is get on a train! Don't tell me you don't want to go to Paris!"

13

George, who had waved our customer off, came back to the counter. "What's going on?" he asked.

"Nothing much," I said. "Your sister and I are just off on a day trip to Paris, that's all."

CHAPTER THREE

The First Six Problems

"I have a minor problem with this plan," I said to Ruth four minutes later. "Eurostar's fully booked. We're going to have to fly."

"Well I have five more problems," said Ruth.

"Like what?"

"One, two and three – I'm looking after three kids. Sorry, George, two kids and a brother. Four, I don't think the airline will want to fly all these groceries. And five, I don't have a ticket. Apart from that, I'm with you all the way."

"I can come too," said George. Then he made a face. "Except I'm supposed to be going round to Danny's soon."

"George . . ." I began, and then I couldn't think what to say next.

Fortunately, George interrupted me before he had time to notice that I'd stopped. "I really want to go to Danny's," he said, apologetically, "his Dad's going to let us make a horror movie with his camcorder. Sorry, Jo."

"That's all right George," I said generously. "I don't suppose Paris is your kind of place."

15

"Terrific," said Ruth, not sounding terrific at all. "Now I just have the four problems!" She made a face at me. "Send me a postcard," she said, "if you have time. But not the Eiffel Tower – be imaginative."

"We *can't* give up that easily," I said.

I threw myself into the back office to break the news of the project to Dad. He was on the telephone, though, and it didn't seem wise to interrupt. I threw myself back into the front office again.

Peggy had just finished with her customer and was beginning to try and play 'I-Spy' with the twins.

While they were shouting out the names of things beginning with D, I got her attention for long enough to explain what I'd promised.

She looked quite blank, which was unusual for her.

"Dinosaur," yelled the twins, both together.

"No," said Peggy, "it has to be something you can see. What does your father say?"

I said I didn't think he could see a dinosaur from where he was sitting.

"Dog!" shrieked the twins, ignoring the inconvenient fact that there wasn't a dog in sight either.

"Try desk," said George, but they were shouting too loudly to hear.

"I meant, does he agree?" said Peggy to me.

"I'm telling him in a minute," I said. "I *have* to go, I promised the client. Peggy, will you help me? Can you find out if it's possible to get there and back today? Can you find out flight times?"

"Dinner!" bellowed the twins. "Duck!"

"Who's paying for this?" said Peggy.

"Ruth has airmiles," I said, "and me – " I waved my arm about in a casual sort of way, "the firm

16

will pay for me. Under the heading of Customer Relations."

"Desk!" said George to the Munchkins. "Desk, desk, desk, what's the matter with you, it's desk. Now – I spy something beginning with T."

"Ty – rann – o – saur – us," chanted the twins.

"Sure!" said George. "I think there's one behind the counter."

"You're not leaving those two with me, are you?" said Peggy nervously, beginning to dial a number.

"No," said Ruth, "I have to do something about them. Is it okay if I use the other phone? I can call their grandma."

"Twins!" shrieked one of the Munchkins.

"Good try, but no," said George.

Peggy was already through to the airline, so I told Ruth to go ahead and talk to Grandma.

I don't know how she managed it, what with all the shouts of tail and toad and tiger going on all around her. But then I don't know how the twins managed not to guess telephone when they were actually watching two people with receivers clamped to their ears.

I ran back to look at Dad again, but he was still in the same position on his own phone – except that now he was tapping at his calculator with his free hand. It looked important. I hoped it wouldn't go on for too long.

Ruth hung up as I got back to the desk. She looked a bit crushed.

"No good?" I said.

"I tell you what," said George to the twins. "*You* think of a letter and *I'll* guess it."

"Their grandma's getting straight into her car and coming to pick them up," said Ruth.

"A!" screamed one twin. "Zed!" squawked the other.

"So that just leaves the groceries and George?" I said, wondering why Ruth didn't look more cheerful.

"The groceries are for the twins' parents anyway. She'll take them too. And she'll drop George at Danny's on her way back."

"I want Zed!"

"So what's the problem?"

"I *knew* it," said Ruth, pushing her hands through her hair and rattling her beads. "I *knew* it wasn't a proper job."

"I want Wubble-you."

"She's always had them before," said Ruth, raising her voice against the background noise, "she loves having them, for some reason. Everyone was just trying to be nice to me, pretend I had a job, pretend I was needed. I bet she's been sitting at home just *longing* for me to give up."

I said, "Are you completely mad? She's giving you a chance to go to Paris and you're sulking?"

"I have to take things in stages," said Ruth, glaring at me. "First I'll sulk. Then I'll get excited."

"I give up," said George, sounding about fifty years older than he really is. "What can either of you see that begins with Z – or W?"

If there was one thing the twins were agreed on it was that George had to think of words beginning with zed or wubble-you. As far as they were concerned that was his problem, not theirs.

"What about these airmiles?" called Peggy, her

18

hand over the mouthpiece of the receiver. "I need details."

"They're my godmother's," said Ruth, "but she said I could use them."

"If they're hers, she has to get on to the company," said Peggy.

"What company?" said Ruth.

"Airmiles. Airmiles is a company. Your godmother can hand over the miles she's earned, but she has to confirm the booking."

"She may be abroad somewhere, mayn't she?" I said, a feeling of doom coming over me.

"Also, she may not think it's such a good idea to burn all those miles just to spend a few hours in Paris looking for a strange woman who isn't even capable of checking her own equipment," said Ruth, picking up the phone again.

I went for another look at Dad. Nothing had changed.

By the time I got back, Peggy was pulling the twins off George and Ruth was beginning to grin.

"Yes?" I said. "Yes? Yes? Yes?"

"My godmother isn't abroad," said Ruth, "she's in England, at her desk, even. She says the whole idea is totally crazy . . ."

I stood quietly while she enjoyed her dramatic pause.

". . . and she *loves* it," said Ruth. "She's going to call Airmiles right away."

"Brilliant!" I said. "Brilliant, brilliant, but I still can't get Dad's attention."

"Peggy seems to be sorting everything," said Ruth.

"Or she was till the creatures-from-another-planet decided to have a go at George."

"Yes, but Dad has to agree."

"Ask your mum, isn't she upstairs?"

"It has to be him," I said, "it's to do with his company, not Mum's."

"I've just thought," said Ruth. "What about *my* mother?"

"What about her?"

"I think it would be fair just to mention it before we go, don't you?"

I passed her the phone.

The street door opened and I spun round to stare as a grey-haired woman in a pink tracksuit came in. The last thing we needed at this crucial stage was a customer.

The twins flung themselves at her.

"This is their grandma," said George, somewhat unnecessarily, as they hugged her legs. You'd have thought they were the ones about to be rescued from torment, not us.

"We've all been playing 'I-Spy' with them," I said loudly, in case the pink tracksuit thought we hadn't been nice to them.

"You *are* clever," said Grandma admiringly. "I can never get them to do it properly – they're always on about dinosaurs and tigers and things they can't possibly spy."

"Mom, can you hold on?" said Ruth down the phone, and hurried to help George and Grandma get everything and everyone outside and into the car, which was parked at the kerb.

"It's good of you to have them," she said as they bundled out of the door.

"Nonsense," said Grandma, "I've just been sitting at home missing them."

"I think I guessed that," said Ruth.

Everything seemed weirdly quiet when Ruth came back in. Even the other phone ringing seemed gentle – peaceful.

Ruth went to pick up the receiver she'd left lying on the desk. She put her hand over the mouthpiece and hissed at me, "Mom's raising objections." She took her hand off the mouthpiece again and said, "Mom, just think about it for a minute . . ."

"Tell her about Philippe," I whispered.

"Oh yes," said Ruth. "Jo's reminding me to tell you about Philippe, that French exchange student who was over last year? Well he's kind of chunky and dark and very cute . . ."

"Not *that*, you fool," I said, "tell her about all the trips he does for his father's travel firm. Tell her if she won't let you do the same she's being sexist."

"Ruth, I have your godmother on this line," called Peggy, who was on the other phone. "I think there's a hitch."

Ruth dumped her receiver on the desk, ignoring the fact that her mother's voice was still coming out of it, and moved over to the one Peggy was holding.

I didn't even pretend not to listen. In fact I stood right beside her and tried to work out the other half of the conversation.

"Hi again!" said Ruth. Then, "I don't *believe* it . . . oh no, don't worry . . . look, it isn't your fault . . . no, it's okay, it's fine, I'm not disappointed . . . oh, hey, no, you don't have to do that . . . are you sure? . . . well, if it's really okay . . . you're unbelievable! Hey, listen, I promise to look after you when you're old, I'll teach you to do wheelies in your wheelchair . . . okay, yes, right, I'll tell Peggy . . ." She handed back the receiver. "You have to give fourteen days' notice to book Airmiles," she said, "but my godmother's going to pay for my flight!"

"That's very generous of her," said Peggy calmly.

"She says if you don't mind calling her with the details when we're booked, she'll put it on her credit card," said Ruth. "Hey, I've just thought, can we hold the phones together so my godmother can convince my biological mother?"

"No," said Peggy firmly, hanging up. "We do have to keep some lines clear in case there's a genuine customer out there with money to spend."

"Okay," said Ruth, picking up the other phone again. "Mom, listen to me, your best friend is on my side."

"Jo," said Peggy, "pass me that folder, will you. I have to organise insurance for you two and the camera and we haven't got long if you're going to get over and back today *and* have any time in Paris."

I grabbed the file and passed it across. At the same time, Ruth put down her receiver and spun round, hair flying, positively beaming. "It's okay, we're on!" she said.

"See what we can do when we try!" I said. "It was *meant*. Right from the start. I'm really beginning to believe it now! In a couple of hours we'll be standing on French soil."

"I have to run," said Ruth.

"What? Where? We're going together."

"I know, but I have to get home first."

"Ruth, we are going for about four hours, you do *not* need to pack."

"I know that, but I might like to change."

"I'd definitely like to change, but there's no *time*!"

"But I need my passport," said Ruth. "Don't I?"

I stared at her in horror. How could I have forgotten something so basic.

"Mine's kept in the safe in the upstairs office," I said weakly.

"Yes, well mine isn't," said Ruth.

"Is this the sixth problem?" I wailed.

"No," said Ruth. "I can get it, I'll run. I should have taken a ride back with the twins' grandma, but it's okay, I'm fast. How long have I got, Peggy? When do we need to leave?"

"In about ten minutes, I'd say," said Peggy.

"What's in about ten minutes?" said Dad, walking in from the back office.

I explained what we were going to do. I explained it briefly, clearly and efficiently. Later, Ruth said she'd never heard me sound so confident.

And Dad said, "Forget it, we don't offer that kind of service, it's not practical."

I said, "What?"

"You heard," said Dad calmly. "I said *no*."

Ruth looked at me. "Now *that*," she said, "*is* the sixth problem!"

CHAPTER FOUR

The Dogsbody Takes Flight

Dad took the silver case through into the back office, opened it and shook his head at it. "We'd better phone the girl who brought this in," he said, "and tell her to take it right out again."

I might have given up then, but Ruth kept me going.

"I'll jog home for my passport anyway," she whispered in my ear. "Meet you at the subway in twenty minutes. If you don't show after half an hour I'll know it's all off." And then she was gone.

So I started in on Dad.

Neither of us was shouting, but somehow Mum and Bill realised something was going on and came downstairs to see what it was. They seemed more impressed by the lenses than by my project. "This is professional stuff," said Mum, in hushed tones.

"I promised," I said. "I promised I'd get it out there today."

"This is not a service we offer," said Dad again. "No one does."

"If we chased every client who forgot a camera, we'd go broke," said Bill.

24

"This is no ordinary camera!" I said.

Bill shook his head. "You're going to have to face the cruel truth," he said. "You and Paris aren't going to meet today."

"Clair Aitken *is* a very good customer of ours," said Peggy, from the doorway. "I've checked."

Dad looked at her in amazement. "Surely you're not going along with this nonsense, Peggy?" he said.

"It's been a little difficult to concentrate in here for the last half hour or so," said Peggy, using her most dignified voice, "but I do seem to be rather heavily involved with it, yes."

Dad pushed me through into the front of the shop, shunting Peggy ahead of us, leaving my mother and Bill admiring the photography kit. He was going to turn me down – but not in front of Bill.

As soon as we were out of earshot of the back office he said, "Jo, you had no authority to make that promise."

"I know," I said, "but I did make it, and I have to keep it."

"It's madness," said Dad.

I was suddenly absolutely certain that I couldn't bear not to go. I felt as though my mind was already in Paris, all I had to do was make sure my body joined it. Also – and this bit may have been childish – I couldn't bear the thought of Bill being proved right. I decided desperate action was called for.

"I *am* eighteen . . ." I said.

"I hadn't forgotten," said Dad drily. "Your birthday was only last week!"

". . . which means I'm an adult," I said, "and *that* means you can't stop me. All you can do is fire me."

Dad stared at me. "You *are* desperate!" he said.

"She's been working very hard all summer," said Peggy, from behind him. "It isn't the best fun in the world being the dogsbody."

"She's here to work, not have fun," said Dad. "Anyway, we're too late to book return flights for today. There won't be any seats available."

"They're holding two returns," said Peggy. "I have to confirm within the next fifteen minutes."

"And if you do," said Dad, "I'll end up a couple of hundred pounds poorer."

"Ruth's godmother's paying for her," I said, "and you can take my bit out of my salary."

"No I can't, I don't pay you enough."

"Peggy," I said, "you are my witness. My father admits he doesn't pay me enough!"

"I pay you what you're worth," said Dad, beginning to grin.

"Listen," I said, "you stand to win a grateful regular customer *and* a grateful daughter."

I could see he was wavering.

"There'll be me and Ruth together, for just half a day, in a major European city that's no further away than Edinburgh. What could possibly go wrong?"

"*Ruth* isn't eighteen yet," said Dad.

"She will be in five weeks – and she's used to travelling – she goes to her father for a month every year."

"The only place Ruth travels," said Dad, "is to New York, and her mother puts her on the plane this end and her father meets her at the other."

"That's okay, I promise I won't let her fly to JFK by mistake. And we *know* people there – we know

Philippe and you know his parents, and they're tour operators, after all."

"If you're so desperate to see Paris," said Dad, "why don't you save up and go for a weekend?"

"Because it would take ages and ages and I want to go *now*. When I go to bed tonight I want to have memories of garlic and boulevards, not . . . not . . . twin gremlins and brochure racks."

Dad looked thoughtful.

I explained about all the things Ruth had had to arrange, and how easily it had all worked out, and I told him it must be meant. Dad was around in the 60s and 70s – he goes for things being meant.

In ten minutes I was staggering towards the door with the silver case in one hand and my passport, Ruth's and my travel documents, and all-too-few francs among the shredded tissues and loose peppermints in my bag.

Bill said, "Jo, I underestimated your powers of persuasion." Then he winked and added, "Give my love to Paris."

Mum said, "Take this," and shoved a guidebook under my arm.

Dad said, "You'd better make this an efficient operation or you'll never get round me again, not ever."

Peggy said, "Here, you can get this changed at the airport," and pushed some money into my free hand.

"What?" I said, stopping to stare at it.

"Don't get excited," said Peggy, all gruff and embarrassed, "it's not much, it's not much at *all* – but it'll help."

"But why should you give it to me?" I said.

Peggy retreated behind her computer. "I know this

is hard to believe," she muttered, "but I was your age, once. Now go. *Go!*"

I ran to the tube station, but the weight of the case meant it was a slow and lumbering run. My hair, which needed washing, kept flopping into my eyes and my least favourite skirt, the truly dreary one, dragged at my legs. I hoped I wouldn't see anyone I knew. Apart from Ruth, of course.

She was waiting exactly where she'd said she'd be. We got our tickets and reached the platform just as the Heathrow train was opening its doors.

"This is a good omen," I said as we got into it. "Things are going to go smoothly."

"Do you want me to take care of the tickets and stuff?" said Ruth. "Just to make sure of that."

"No. I don't lose things. Why does everyone say I lose things?"

"You lost your maths homework three times."

"That was deliberate."

"You also lost a video cassette and two books, and twice you lost your purse."

"Those were accidents – those were things that could have happened to anyone."

"Okay," said Ruth. "Sorry. Forget it. I trust you."

"Oh yuck," I said, looking down at myself. "Why do I have to decide to go to the home of *haute couture* looking so disgusting?"

"You look better than you think you do."

"That wouldn't be hard."

"I know what happens," said Ruth, as the train rocked through the tunnels. "Here's the story. You come back from Paris, all sophisticated, in a designer outfit, and Bill doesn't recognise you and he says,

'Hey, who *is* that chick – that chic chick' – and then he realises it's you and he's knocked out and he asks you to dinner and can't take his eyes off you."

She stopped because I was shaking my head.

"Okay," she said, "try this – he *asks* you to dinner but you turn him down."

I still shook my head.

"Scornfully?" offered Ruth and then got distracted by the name of the station we were just pulling out of. "Boston Manor!" she said. "Where *are* we? Did we just fly the Atlantic without me knowing?"

"Five more stations," I said.

"Oh," said Ruth, losing interest in our route. "Sorry! I get it! I'm not being politically correct here. *You* ask *Bill* to dinner. And he falls over himself to go out with the new, sophisticated you?"

I looked down at myself. "It'd take more than a few hours in Paris to make me look sophisticated," I said.

"A designer outfit," said Ruth. "I *said* there'd be a designer outfit."

"I don't know if my francs are going to stretch to pommes frites," I said, "I'd have to save for a year to buy the spare button off a designer outfit."

"You take things so literally," said Ruth. "I'm fantasising here – come over on to my planet for a minute, why don't you? I'm just trying to find out if you fancy Bill."

"No – I don't know – I haven't decided. I think *you* do, though. But you've got Gareth."

"Gareth's fine for everyday," said Ruth. "Bill would be more of an exciting interlude. *Hey*, I've just thought of something *awful*."

"What! *What*?"

"I'm travelling on an American passport – don't I need a visa or something?"

"No, you don't."

"Are you sure?"

"Yes, I am sure, and don't give me frights, I'm nervous enough already."

"Why are you nervous?" said Ruth, startled. "You know Paris, don't you?"

"I've been there," I said guardedly.

"Well, that's what I said," said Ruth.

"Yes, but I wasn't on my own that time," I said. I flipped through the guidebook Mum had given me, trying to find the bit that tells you what to do when you get to the airport.

"You're not on your own this time," said Ruth, "you have me!"

"And how well do *you* know Paris?"

"Give me a chance, I've only been in the UK for seven years!" said Ruth. "Though my godmother did send me a postcard of Notre Dame once. Or maybe it was the Paris Opera House, I forget."

"I can see you're going to be a huge help."

"But it doesn't matter what *I* know," said Ruth. "I'm not taking you – you're taking me."

"So I am," I said, getting up. "Here's our stop."

Ruth followed me as I strode importantly around the Terminal building, determined not to hesitate or look lost even for a second. I thought I bluffed very well, especially as I got us to the departure lounge just as the flight was called, which meant we could board at once.

I relaxed as the plane taxied down the runway, silently congratulating myself.

Then Ruth said, "Don't panic. It's going to be okay."

"Who's panicking?"

"You. You dropped your passport, you dropped the tickets, you dropped the boarding passes, the only thing you didn't drop was Clair's kit."

"I was just worried about letting the films go through the x-ray," I said.

"You're worried about more than that!" said Ruth. "Just exactly how familiar *are* you with Paris?"

"I don't claim to know every single street."

"How many times have you been?"

"And I don't claim to go regularly."

"Jo, *how many times*?"

"Once."

"With your parents?"

"Yes."

"And how long did you stay?"

"We went to other places as well as Paris," I said defensively.

"How long in Paris?"

"It's a compact city," I said. "You can see a lot in a short time."

"*How long*? How many nights?"

I didn't answer.

"Okay," said Ruth, "so you didn't stop over. You're telling me you've only ever spent one day in Paris, right?"

"Most of a day," I said.

"And how long ago was this?"

"Couple of years," I muttered.

The plane screamed down the runway and lifted off. I looked out of the window and watched as it tilted, pointing briefly at the ground with one wing tip. "They must hate us," I said, "all those people in the houses down there. They must hate the noise we make."

"Don't change the subject," said Ruth. "Listen, you don't have to bluff me. I'm on your side."

"Sorry," I said.

I looked at Ruth properly for the first time since she'd sprinted off for her passport. She was still wearing the same jeans and top. She'd been home, she could have changed – but she hadn't because she knew I couldn't. She was right, she was on my side. It seemed only fair to tell her what I was thinking.

"This seemed such a brilliant idea back in the office," I said, "and I thought I wouldn't be able to bear it if we couldn't come. But now we're actually up in the air, it all seems a bit extreme suddenly."

"It'll be fine," said Ruth. "Relax. We'll call Philippe from the airport and he's sure to come out and meet us. He'll know where the hotel is, so we'll be able to go straight there, dump the case, and have a great time for a few hours. Simple."

"What if," I said, "Clair Aitken is already out and about in Paris, trying to take photos through the wrong lenses?"

"Not our problem," said Ruth. "You promised to get the case to her hotel and we will. After that, it's up to her. Anyway, the girl who came into the office will have called to say you're on your way. Clair'll probably be hanging around in the lobby waiting to grab it from you."

"And after that," I said, "we find the best restaurant we can afford."

"Right!" said Ruth. "Let's not eat up here – let's save ourselves for French food."

"Definitely," I said. And I began to enjoy myself again.

The stewardess came down the aisle, smiling and handing out plastic trays, but we waved her away.

"Look at them all," said Ruth, rearing up in her seat to stare along the body of the plane, "eating pre-packed food on the way to Paris! What's the matter with them? They have no style."

"We have style," I said.

"We have style with a dash of panáche," said Ruth.

"Dashing but not flashy," I said.

"Not flash and not rash," said Ruth.

"Oh, I like to think we're rash," I said. "Yes, we're definitely rash. We're the wild women dropping out of the skies onto Paris just because we feel like it."

"Your spirits have certainly gone up," said Ruth.

"Right up," I said. "My spirits and I are about three thousand feet up."

"My spirits and I are with you," said Ruth, "and ready to handle any problems we may meet."

"We won't meet any problems," I said. "I hereby declare Paris a problem-free zone."

Unfortunately, Paris didn't seem to understand that.

CHAPTER FIVE

The Right People are not in Town

The thing about arriving in a foreign city by plane is that you *think* you're there the moment the wheels bounce on the runway, but in fact there's an awful lot you still have to do. Like queuing up to get off because the plane's full and you've been in the cheap seats at the back. Like going through customs and immigration. Like finding your way out of the airport. Like travelling from the airport into the city centre.

Looking back, I can see it all went quite quickly, especially as we'd been able to take the case on as hand luggage, which cut out the bit where you hang around the carousel waiting for it, but at the time it seemed like a lot of work.

We decided to ring Philippe at once, before we left the airport. We found a payphone. Then we found somewhere to buy a phonecard. Eventually we went back to the payphone with the phonecard.

We stood close together, the receiver jammed between my left ear and Ruth's right ear, and the silver case jammed between my left foot and Ruth's right foot.

"Somehow I don't think we look like a pair of sophisticated business-women," I said.

"Shut up and call the number," said Ruth.

I lost my nerve as soon as the phone was answered. "Do you speak English?" I asked hopefully in French. The man at the other end of the line did speak English, which was nice. What was less nice was that he told me that Philippe was away with his father and a group of tourists in Thailand. He gave me their home number so we could call Philippe's mother, but there didn't seem any point in writing it down. Phoning a friend to say, "Hey, come and meet us, let's hang out together" is one thing. Phoning his mother to ask for help is something entirely different.

"We should have guessed he might be off somewhere," I complained to Ruth. "Why didn't we?"

"It doesn't matter," Ruth said firmly, as we walked away from the phone. "We don't need him. We can crack it ourselves."

That was when we discovered that we were lost in the airport.

We were walking along a curved corridor with blank walls and no exit doors. It seemed to go on forever.

"What did we do?" said Ruth. "There was a whole planeload of us walking in line through customs and immigration – where'd everyone else disappear to?"

"They're going to be really impressed at home when they hear we couldn't even get out of the airport," I said.

"Keep walking," said Ruth.

"It's all right for you," I said, trying not to whine, but failing. "This case is gravitationally challenged.

35

I'm not going to be able to keep it off the ground for much longer."

"I'll carry it," said Ruth.

"No. It's my turn."

"I'd rather do double-turn than hear you moaning," said Ruth sharply. Then she stopped abruptly and a smile spread across her face. "Hey," she said, "we have travel-stress, right? That *is* executive stuff."

"I don't think I want the executive image at the moment," I said. "I think I want to be carefree. I certainly don't want to be lost."

"Remember what you said before," said Ruth, "back in the office. You said it's important to look as though you know what you're doing. Well, we don't. We look like two trainee ferrets lost in a rabbit warren."

"What does it matter – there's no one to see us."

"You have to kid the universe you can cope," said Ruth. "If it thinks you're worried it just goes on bullying you. We've got to get a grip."

We both knew she was right.

We stood still. We straightened our shoulders. We took a deep breath each. We relaxed our eyebrows. We smiled at each other. Then – confident, calm, casual – we strolled on. And within seconds we were walking through wide doors to a large and draughty porch-area where the last passengers were just boarding the shuttlebus for the train-station.

"See," said Ruth, "it works!"

The station, when we got there, was a confusion of noise and crowds, but I'd read the relevant page of the guidebook on the shuttlebus and I managed to get us onto the RER suburban express into Paris.

We sat back and tried hard to get excited by the view from the windows.

"Very industrial, isn't it," said Ruth.

"We haven't got to the good bit yet," I said.

"I guessed that," said Ruth.

Later she said, "What'll we do when we get to the good bit?"

"We'll *flâner*," I said.

"We'll *what*?"

"It's French," I said. "It's a French word and it's a French thing to do. It means stroll, wander, drift where the mood takes you."

"You're saying it's French for 'hang out'?" said Ruth.

"Yup."

"And where will we *flâner*?"

"When you're a *flâneur*," I said, "the whole point is you don't make plans. But we'll take in markets and cafés, we'll see Notre Dame and the Paris Opera House, we're bound to see the Eiffel Tower, we ought to take a look at the Louvre, and we'll definitely *flâner* by the Seine."

"How long is all this going to take?" said Ruth. "Do you realise it'll be almost three by the time we hit this hotel? And I have just had my fourteenth hunger-pang."

I said, "Paris is an evening city. The flight home isn't till nine-thirty."

As soon as the RER got anywhere near the interesting bits of the city, it plunged underground.

"I've seen Paris from above," said Ruth, as we rattled along, "and I'm seeing quite a lot of it from underneath. I hope I get a look at it from ground level before I leave."

I only half heard what she said. I'd been working something out. "Ruth," I said, "are you super-stitious?"

"I don't know," said Ruth cautiously. "Why?"

"We had six problems before we even started," I said, "and now we're here we've had three already." I counted on my fingers. "One: Philippe being away, two: getting lost in the airport, three: going past our station. Do you suppose that means there are going to be three more?"

"Those weren't *problems*," said Ruth. "Minor hassles, that's all." She stood up because I was stand-ing up. "And, anyway," she said, "we won't go past our station. Is this it?"

The train stopped and I pressed the button to open the door.

"No," I said, hitching the case into a more comfortable position, "we wanted the one before."

"Why didn't you *say*?" said Ruth, following me on to the platform.

"I couldn't see the name of the last one. Someone's head was in the way. And I'd lost count. Anyway, why weren't *you* watching – do I have to do everything?"

"You're the travel agent," said Ruth, "you're the European – I thought it was polite to leave it to you."

"You've never been polite to me before," I said. "Don't start now! I plan to cross over and get a train back one stop. Don't let me do it wrong."

"You got it," said Ruth. We struggled on in silence, afraid of losing concentration again.

Fortunately it didn't take too long to get back to

the right station. Before we left it, I bought us a *carnet* of ten tickets.

"I'm back in control now," I said to Ruth. "I've equipped us for all transportation needs. We can use these on the Metro or the buses."

"Good," said Ruth. "Don't lose them."

"It's a *myth* that I lose things."

"Okay," said Ruth, as we climbed up to street level, "I just didn't want them to be the next problem. I think you could be right, we could be developing a tradition here, with six as the key number."

"No," I said, "forget it – those three weren't real problems."

The fourth was, though.

The first bit was all right. We followed the map in the back of the guidebook and after a couple of streets we saw the hotel sign, just where it should have been.

We were in classy, right-bank Paris. The buildings looked foreign, the signs were in French, there was even a bakery stocked with baguettes just across the road.

The fact that London is full of bakeries stocked with baguettes didn't bother me at all. Here they were in their native country. They would be bound to taste different. I was sure they smelt different. I couldn't actually smell them at that moment because they were the other side of four lanes of heavy traffic – but that didn't bother me either. It was French traffic, with French number-plates and French fumes, and therefore far more interesting than English traffic.

"We've done it," I said, "we've really done it, we're actually here."

We swung down the road to the entrance. We strode into the lobby. I led the way up to the desk. Ruth was taking her turn with the case, and anyway I'm the one who's supposed to be able to speak French.

I did not let myself be put off by the hostile glare of the receptionist. I did not let myself be dazzled by her heavy gold jewellery, or by the fact that she seemed to have recently fallen into a giant bottle of perfume.

Speaking up and speaking clearly, in French, I informed her that we had come to see a guest at the hotel. I gave her the name and, just to be sure, placed on the desk in front of her a piece of paper on which I had taken the precaution of printing it out.

I could tell she didn't like me by the extra-slow way she checked through the hotel records. Also by the unpleasant way she smiled when she gave me the news.

"There is no one," she said in perfect English, "of the name of Clair Aitken staying at this hotel."

And she turned away from me and began to attend to the next customer.

CHAPTER SIX

The Power Women

When the receptionist said no one of the name of Clair Aitken was booked in at the hotel, my first thought wasn't that the project seemed to have failed before it had started. My first thought was that I was hungry. My *second* thought was that the project seemed to have failed before it had started.

I tried to catch the attention of the receptionist again to ask her if there was another hotel in Paris with the same name. By now she was on the telephone. She ignored me.

Ruth pulled at my sleeve. "We have the address," she said. "This has to be the place."

"What can we do?" I wailed.

"Eat?" said Ruth.

"Yes, but we have to get rid of this case first. I'm going to phone home."

There was a polished wooden phone booth at the back of the lobby, next to some dusty drapes. It took coins. I put away our phonecard and we both piled all the coins we had on the little wooden shelf, all ready. Then I called Quest Travel.

Peggy checked with the records, while I hung on.

"No, you're all right," she said at last, "you're in the right hotel."

"Could the room have been booked under a company name?" I said.

"All the bookings with us have been made under the name Clair Aitken," said Peggy. "Don't worry – we have a London address and telephone number here – your father's calling it now in case there's anyone there who can throw any light."

She tried to make conversation with me while we waited, but I couldn't concentrate, and anyway I had nothing to tell her.

At last she broke off.

I heard Dad's voice in the background.

Then Peggy said, "Your father says there's no reply."

"Isn't there a work address?" I said. "Can't we call that girl?"

"This is the only address we have," said Peggy. "I should think most photographers are freelance, aren't they? Don't they usually work from home?"

"Well if there's a studio at home," I said, "that must be where that girl works. Why doesn't she answer?"

"Probably out getting something to eat," muttered Ruth, beside me.

"Jo," said Peggy, down the phone, "your father says it's not your responsibility. It never was. You've delivered the case to the address you were given. Now leave it at the desk and forget about it. It's up to Clair Aitken to pick it up from there. Go and enjoy Paris – and don't use all your money on the telephone."

In order to make sure I couldn't, she hung up on me.

The lobby, which had been almost empty when we arrived, was getting busier. The doors to the small dining room had been propped open and people were beginning to wander out – having just eaten a long and good lunch, I assume.

"So can we abandon Ms Aitken and get on with things?" said Ruth, when I'd passed on the other half of the conversation.

"No, how can we? Now we've interfered in her life we have a responsibility to her, whatever Dad and Peggy say. What about sisterhood?"

"But she may not even *be* in Paris," said Ruth. "She may have changed her mind and jetted off somewhere else."

"We know she should be in *this* hotel. Peggy's confirmed it."

"Yes, but she's not going to phone Peggy and announce she's decided to dump the hotel and go visit her lover in Geneva, or wherever, is she? She'd just do it."

"Let's have one more try," I said. "You have a go at that receptionist. She didn't like me, she didn't like the way I was dressed, I could tell."

"She won't like me any better," said Ruth.

At that moment a tall thin man appeared behind the desk. He had a fistful of letters which he began to push into individual pigeon-holes.

"Try him," said Ruth.

I went back to the desk. "Good afternoon," I said, loudly and importantly, "I am from Quest Travel in

London, and I have a case to deliver to Clair Aitken, who I believe is staying here."

The tall thin man drifted towards me. He managed to look surprised and faintly disgusted at the same time – as if a piece of litter had unexpectedly fluttered up from the floor and spoken to him. He fired a lot of rapid French at me, using an unnecessary number of words to ask me what I wanted.

I let him have it again, this time in French. I added that Clair Aitken would almost certainly have been carrying a case that looked exactly like the one I was holding. He was as slow with the register as the perfumed woman had been, but his answer was different. "Yes," he said in English, "a room has been reserved in that name, but, as my colleague told you, Mlle Aitken has not arrived. She did not – as you would say – check in. If someone else requires the room I fear we shall be obliged to permit them to reserve it."

He walked away and went back to sorting the mail.

Before I had time to ask Ruth what she thought of that, two smartly-dressed, middle-aged Australian women came up to us.

"Did I hear you say you're from Quest Travel?" said the one who reached us first.

I said I was.

"Well, I'm Mrs Cooper and this is Mrs Mackenzie," said Mrs Cooper, "and we're not very pleased to find that you've booked us into very noisy rooms at the front of the hotel. Will you kindly arrange to have us moved to rooms at the back."

Some people have such an air of authority that you obey before you realise you don't have to. Mrs

Cooper was one of them. I returned to the desk and accosted the perfumed receptionist at once.

I spoke in French. She replied in English. I wasn't surprised. I'd learnt the pattern by now.

Mrs Cooper and Mrs Mackenzie kept a dignified distance during the negotiations. This gave Ruth a chance to ask them if by chance they'd flown out from London. They had. Might they, she went on, just possibly, have come out on the same flight as Clair Aitken. They hadn't. What was more, they were shocked to hear that such early flights existed. They seemed even more shocked that anyone should think they might have taken an interest in their fellow passengers.

While the receptionist reluctantly agreed to change their rooms, they told Ruth they had neither spoken to nor noticed anyone else on their flight, with or without a silver camera-case. There simply hadn't been time, they said, what with drinks and meals being served and then cleared away again.

I interrupted to give them the good news about the room changes.

"You're more efficient than you look," said Mrs Cooper. She didn't smile.

As she and Mrs Mackenzie stalked off with their new keys, a man closed in on us from the other side. As Ruth said later, it takes true style to look as scruffy as he did while wearing a seriously good suit, clean shirt and polished shoes. It had to do with his hair, which was definitely shaggy, and his face, which was so untidily made it was almost ugly – but only almost.

"May I introduce myself," he said, with just enough of a French accent to make his voice as stylishly untidy as the rest of him. "I am Jean Deguand. I couldn't help overhearing your conversation and I thought I should tell you that I sat next to Clair Aitken on the flight over. I remember because of the unusual name – and because the Scottish accent was a problem for me."

CHAPTER SEVEN

The Essential Paris

"This is great!" said Ruth with such enthusiasm that Jean Deguand took a very small step backwards – but only a very small one. "Someone who knows the mysterious Clair Aitken!"

"We've brought this case from London," I said, feeling that M. Deguand deserved some kind of explanation, "and we need to hand it over but we can't seem to make contact . . ."

Jean Deguand smiled and held up his hands as if to defend himself. "I cannot help much more, alas," he said. "I was almost the last to leave the plane – I prefer to allow the rush to die down – and as I got up I saw that some papers had been left on the seat beside me. I hurried, then, in the hope of being able to return them – but I was too late. By that time I had looked more carefully and seen that it was only one paper – a map with some small notes – and it did not seem sufficiently important for me to give chase – but it is in my room. Perhaps it would be appropriate for me to give it to you?"

"It might help," I said. "There might be an address of somewhere we could take this case."

He made a little gesture with his hand to indicate we should wait – and strolled off towards the gilded lift.

"We're getting somewhere!" I said to Ruth.

"I don't know where!" said Ruth. "He doesn't know where Clair is, either."

"No," I said, "but we know she definitely caught the plane and she definitely reached Paris. And there may be a clue in the notes."

"This is getting out of hand," said Ruth. "It isn't our responsibility any more, your father said so."

"Well, we have to wait till M. Deguand comes back," I said. I nudged her. "He might offer to show us Paris."

"You wish!" said Ruth, beginning to giggle.

"And anyway," I said, "seriously, Ruth, we have to do something. Don't you realise, we're the only people who know she's missing."

"Just because she hasn't checked in," said Ruth, "doesn't mean she's missing. It's not three-thirty yet."

"The hotel thinks she's missing," I said.

"The hotel doesn't want to encourage two hobos like us to hang around in its lobby," said Ruth. "They want rid of us – that's why they're being hostile. They're not *really* going to let the room go."

"But she caught a six-thirty flight," I said. "She's been over here for hours and hours."

"So – she decided to sightsee on the way from the airport."

"Carrying all her luggage?"

"She may be travelling light."

"Admit it," I said, "it *is* odd."

48

"It is a *bit* odd," said Ruth reluctantly. "What is also odd is why those women couldn't change their own rooms."

"Those are power women," I said. "They're used to having everything done for them. Those are the kind of women who walk straight *at* a door, knowing someone's bound to open it for them before they reach it."

"If they walked *at* a door around where we live," said Ruth, "they'd walk smack into it."

"These women would never, ever, hang out around where we live."

"Stand up straight," said Ruth, "and try to look beautiful. He's on his way back."

Jean Deguand approached us, smiling sadly. "I am sorry," he said, holding out a map, which had been folded all inside out and backwards. "Now I look more carefully I think perhaps this was left behind because it is debris."

I took it from him and looked at it. It was a map of Paris, which is what you'd expect, but it had scribbles in one of the margins. When I looked at them, though, they didn't seem to mean anything. There was hardly any writing, just little drawings – doodles really. All the visible edges of the map were partly shredded.

"Your friend Clair is a very nervous traveller," said Jean Deguand.

"Thank you anyway . . ." Ruth began and then broke off as the doors of the gilded lift opened and Mrs Cooper and Mrs Mackenzie emerged.

Each now had a lightweight coat slung casually around the shoulders of her smart dress, each had a handbag over one arm, each carried gloves. Behind them, but obviously with them, was a tall blond guy of about twenty, in jeans and a sweatshirt, who looked as though he'd come straight off the nearest beach.

"Good grief, they're sharing a toy-boy," Ruth hissed in my ear.

They didn't make for the street door, as I'd expected, they walked straight up to us. For some reason I began to feel anxious. I was right to.

"We're ready," said Mrs Cooper. Then, when I looked blank, she added, "What's been planned for our afternoon?"

Jean Deguand smiled at us sympathetically and said, "I can see you are busy. If you permit, I will store the camera bag in my room for you. I have no commitments until later this evening. It can be collected from me whenever it is needed."

Mrs Cooper and Mrs Mackenzie completely ignored him, which I thought was surprising, even for middle-aged women with a blond bombshell in tow.

"We should be starting shortly," said Mrs Cooper, and Mrs Mackenzie nodded. "The afternoon is running out on us."

"I need to *eat*," Ruth hissed in my ear.

I thought I was magnificent.

To Jean Deguand I said, "Thank you very much, but I think we must leave the case at reception."

To Mrs Cooper, Mrs Mackenzie and their extraordinarily good-looking companion I said, "I'm afraid we're not here officially, we just came over to deliver something. I'm sure the hotel will be able to provide you with a guidebook."

To Ruth I said, "Me too, let's go."

Jean Deguand smiled and moved away, but before we could do the same, Mrs Cooper whisked out a bunch of Quest Travel literature from her bag and pushed it at me. "It says here," she said, " 'morning: at leisure – afternoon: three-hour tour of the city, entry fees not included'."

Even then, I was still in control.

Calmly, I examined the papers.

Clearly I explained that she and Mrs Mackenzie were not on a Quest Tour, they had simply booked their flight and hotel through Quest Travel. Neither Quest Travel nor Quest Tours was supposed to do anything else for them. What was more, the piece of paper with 'afternoon: tour of the city' on it referred to London.

"Yes, we had a pleasant trip around London," said Mrs Mackenzie, nodding and smiling. "Didn't we, Tom?"

Tom, who was still standing just behind them, looked at me over their heads, crossed his fingers, crossed his eyes, and said, "Yup, terrific!"

"It started *much* earlier than this," said Mrs Cooper.

Mrs Mackenzie must have noticed me looking at Tom because she leaned towards me and said, "It's very good of a young man like Tom to spend time with his boring aunts, don't you think?"

There's no polite way of answering a question like that, but fortunately I didn't have to because Mrs Cooper cut in with, "I really must insist that we get going right away."

What do you do with people who don't listen?

I said, "You have not booked a tour of Paris."

Mrs Cooper frowned at me. "Are you trying to tell me the tour has been cancelled?" she said.

"Not *cancelled*," I said, "it . . ."

"Well, if it isn't cancelled," said Mrs Cooper, "there's no excuse for further delay."

"We are not your couriers," I said.

"Are you specifically refusing to discharge your duties?" said Mrs Cooper.

I spoke loudly and clearly. I said, "It's coincidence that we're here – we have nothing to do with your trip."

I began to move towards the doors as I spoke, but they followed me.

Ruth, not wanting to embarrass me (so she said later), backed off a little way. Possibly Tom felt the same – anyhow, he backed off, too, but in the opposite direction. Facing the power women on my own, I felt smaller and tattier than I'd felt in years. And that was when Mrs Cooper really let me have it.

"I'm not sure," she said, "whether I shall report to your company that you're lazy, or simply that you're incompetent. I must say, your appearance doesn't inspire confidence."

I sidled away from her. She closed in again.

A mixture of rage and hunger fizzed in my stomach. From way behind his aunts, Tom mimed shooting them in the back with a machine-gun.

I would have liked to have followed Tom's suggestion – but unfortunately it wasn't practical. However, if I was at a loss, my voice wasn't. For the second time that day, it spoke all by itself.

"Fine!" it said. "All right!" it said. "We'll take you

on our 'Essential Paris' trip. We leave immediately," it said.

I lugged the silver case across to reception and dumped it by the counter. The perfumed woman had disappeared. The tall thin man watched my approach from the letter rack.

Ruth followed me, hissing, "Are you *crazy*?"

"I'm using my initiative," I said, signalling to the thin man who approached reluctantly.

"Well, I just wish you'd stop doing that!" said Ruth. "We don't want them with us!"

Mrs Cooper and Mrs Mackenzie were already at the lobby door, pulling on their gloves. Tom stood by them, his hands in his pockets.

"We can't get rid of them," I said, "you've seen what they're like, they'll follow us anyway. And one out of three of them could be good company."

"One between us ain't enough," said Ruth acidly. "Anyway, I've got Gareth."

"Well, that's all right then, isn't it?" I said smugly.

Then I explained to the thin man that we would be leaving Clair Aitken's case in his charge for a few hours. Thinking I'd cracked the system, I said it twice – once in French and once in English.

"I am afraid that is out of the question," said the thin man in English. "We cannot take responsibility for the luggage of a person who is not currently a resident."

Before he had time to get back to his letter rack again, Jean Deguand appeared at my side. He stooped and picked up the camera case. "No problem," he said. "I will care for this in my room –

three . . . um . . . two, until it is needed. If I see Clair I will hand it over."

I gripped the edge of the counter. If I looked to my left I could see Jean Deguand and the case disappearing in the direction of the lift. If I looked to my right I could see Mrs Cooper, Mrs Mackenzie and Tom disappearing through the street door, with Ruth right behind them. Was this the fifth problem or the sixth? I'd given up counting.

I had to make an urgent executive decision. I let go of the counter and headed for the street door.

CHAPTER EIGHT

The Best Place

Ruth was looking me straight in the eye as I stumbled out on to the pavement and into the midst of the group. I could read her expression perfectly. It was asking me a question. It was saying, 'Do you know what you're doing or are we in deep trouble here?'

It was not a question I wanted to answer at that exact moment in time, so I looked away from her quickly. That was when I saw Tom was backing off, slowly but definitely, grinning as he went, and doing a kind of apologetic half-wave with both hands.

I just gaped at him, but Ruth said, "Hey, where are you going?"

"I travel with my aunts – I don't sightsee with them," said Tom. Then he winked at me and swung away along the crowded pavement.

It was perfectly obvious that he'd never meant to come with us. It was also perfectly obvious that he'd guessed I thought he would. I was so embarrassed I could almost have cried.

I would like you to know that I didn't, though. I would like you to know that I turned instantly in the opposite direction and set off, fast, calling, "This way, please." If Tom looked back, I wanted him to see me striding confidently off without so much as a glance in his direction. I wanted him to think I was so uninterested in him that I'd already forgotten him.

I hope he did look back, but I'll never know – because I didn't. In fact I led my group rapidly around the first corner so that I couldn't weaken.

Mrs Cooper, pounding along behind my left shoulder – and sounding just a little less pushy than before – said, "Don't you have a car waiting?"

I ignored her and kept going, but I heard good old Ruth say, "You don't drive in Paris! In Paris, you *flâner*!"

Mrs Mackenzie, just behind my right shoulder, said, "Haven't you forgotten something? Shouldn't there be a leaflet for us to study?"

"No, we don't work that way," I said firmly. "It takes the freshness out of a tour if you're reading a leaflet all the time."

Ruth had caught up and was walking beside me now. She was still trying to catch my eye. She was still wanting me to let her in on my plans.

I stared straight ahead.

I had no plans.

I only had a very rough notion of where we were starting out from – I certainly had no idea where I was leading them – and I didn't see how I could possibly look at the guidebook in front of Mrs C and Mrs M.

I was relying totally on the fact that Paris is supposed to be an exciting city. I reasoned that this must mean that if we walked for long enough we were bound to come upon something interesting. One snag, of course, was that even if we did, I probably wouldn't know what it was. Another snag was that my tour group of two were likely to lose patience before we got there – wherever 'there' was. That's why I was walking fast.

I didn't think I could communicate all that to Ruth without speaking, and I wasn't sure how I could speak without being overheard.

"I think you ought to give us some idea of where we're going," said Mrs Cooper. "I hope the Louvre isn't on the agenda. We did the Louvre this morning."

"Don't worry," I said, "we're not going to the Louvre." I tried to ignore the tiny voice in the back of my mind that said, "How do *you* know?"

What I needed, desperately, was to divert their attention for long enough to let me find us on the street map and then check the guidebook. It would have to be quite a big diversion. By now I was so flustered and panicky I would need time to calm down before I could focus. I looked wildly in each direction – saw a meaningless blur of pedestrians, traffic and buildings – and also a bus stop with a bus just pulling up.

"Here we are!" I said, in my most assertive voice, "What perfect timing," and I ushered them all on board.

Ruth's expression changed as I did this. It relaxed. I had convinced her that I knew what I was doing. That helped to relax me a bit, too, not because I *wanted* to fool Ruth but because I knew that if I *could* fool Ruth then I could definitely fool strangers.

I fished out our *carnet* of ten tickets and made an

important business of punching one for each of us in the machine. This turned out to be the single useful thing I remembered from the visit with my parents. However, it was very valuable.

"Well, I must say . . ." said Mrs Cooper, ". . . this is very impressive. You really have to know a city before you can use its public transport system with such confidence."

"Just relax for a few minutes," I said, "and enjoy the view."

They sat together but all the rest of the empty seats were singles. Ruth sat behind them – I was able to go further back and sit on the other side.

I groped in my bag and pulled out what I thought was the guidebook. It wasn't, though, it was Clair's partly-shredded map, which I'd shoved in last. I tried not to let myself be distracted by thoughts of what had become of her – or even by the notes and doodles in the corner which I still hadn't looked at properly. I didn't bother to dig deeper for the guidebook. I knew there wasn't time to work out a thrilling programme of sightseeing. The best I could hope for at that point was to get us somewhere historic where I could dump the two women and get Ruth to help me plan the next move.

I stared out of the window as the bus weaved along its route until I spotted a street name. I struggled with the map, which hadn't been folded properly, until I found the same name on that.

And I thought I understood where we were and what we could do. I thought the bus was heading more or less in the direction of the Louvre (dammit), but that if we got off before we reached it, and took a left, we'd come to the river. Then I could frog-march them along the quayside to Ile de la Cité and Notre Dame. I felt sure the Cathedral would hold their attention while I sorted myself out. I assumed they wouldn't mind glimpsing the Louvre again as long as they didn't have to go into it.

If I'd looked at the map on the wall of the bus itself I might have been all right, but I didn't. That's why I didn't discover at that stage that I'd got myself upside down and back to front.

Even though nothing I could see out of the window seemed to tie in with anything I could see on the map, I was too nervous to understand what had happened. Also, no matter which way I folded the thing, I couldn't find the bit that gave the scale. I had no idea how far we should travel on this bus. I began to develop a horrible mental picture of ending up right outside the city walls.

I panicked, rose to my feet, and said, "We get off here."

Although I was now so totally lost that everything was beginning to look nightmarish, I still believed that I only had to turn left and walk a short way to find the river – maybe not at exactly the point where I'd expected to meet it, but anywhere would do. Although it was a dull day it wasn't cold – I should be able to convince them that a stroll by the Seine was a suitable excursion. I even had a line ready, which went something like: 'I brought you this way because I wanted you to see Notre Dame from this angle.'

So I led us around the first available left turn

and hurried on at speed, keeping ahead to make conversation difficult.

"Which area is this?" said Mrs Cooper, from behind me. She didn't sound suspicious, yet. She was still too impressed about the bus.

"It's a surprise," I said, "I don't want you to have preconceived ideas – I want you to see things as they really are, not as you expect them to be."

My heart was jumping about like a flea and my stomach felt like a washing machine doing a high-speed rinse. I didn't know how much longer I could hope to get away with the bluff, but I thought we were probably down to seconds now, rather than minutes. Especially as I had led us into a cul-de-sac.

The street was blocked at the end by a line of buildings, with an open archway at its centre. Through the archway I thought I could glimpse a lawn – I also thought I could see railings. It seemed highly likely that the archway opened onto something interesting. It seemed equally likely that it was private.

Mrs Mackenzie pointed at the display in a shop window, and she and Mrs Cooper stopped to look at it. While their attention was distracted Ruth came up beside me and grabbed my arm. "Where *are* we going?" she whispered. "You can tell me."

"I can't," I whispered back miserably, hurrying on, "I haven't the least idea. I haven't found us on the map yet."

"*What!*" said Ruth, which caught their attention in the worst possible way.

"What's the problem?" said Mrs Cooper at once, suddenly alert, her voice full of distrust. But before

I had to answer we were at the archway. It was not private, it was open. We passed through the line of buildings. We were in a colonnade which looked on to a wide and beautiful square with dignified buildings around the edges, huge plane trees, formal gravel paths, and a statue of a man on a horse just visible through the leaves.

"There isn't a problem," I said, keeping my voice steady. "Ruth was knocked out by the view, that's all."

"What a magnificent place!" said Mrs Mackenzie.

"Very impressive!" said Mrs Cooper.

I hardly noticed Ruth unhooking my bag from my shoulder. I walked straight out and a little way into the square, and then I revolved slowly as if admiring it. One of the buildings, right in a corner, was obviously 'something'. Three people were coming out holding what looked like a bunch of postcards. One man was going in. I decided to risk it.

"Here we go," I said, and headed straight for it. "We'll wait outside for you."

"This is very exciting," said Mrs Mackenzie, which made me feel a bit guilty. But by then we were at the door and we could all see where we were.

"Victor Hugo's house!" said Mrs Cooper enthusiastically. "This is wonderful – we saw *Les Misérables* in London, you know. Oh well, of course you will know that, I expect Quest Travel booked our theatre seats, and obviously that's why you planned to bring us here. Very well thought out, I must say."

"And this square is delightful," said Mrs Mackenzie.

"Yup," said Ruth, stuffing the guidebook back into

my bag, which she now had over her shoulder. "This is *the* Place – *the* square – the model for all other city squares." She leant closer to me and whispered its name in my ear.

"Place des Vosges," I announced, managing a slightly better pronunciation than Ruth's.

We sagged against each other in relief as Mrs Cooper and Mrs Mackenzie disappeared into the house with expectant smiles on their faces.

Ruth handed me back my bag.

"Thanks," I said. "Thanks for working out where we are. I could have blown it right up to that last second. What a team!"

Ruth glared at me. "Some team!" she said. "Why didn't you tell me you were bluffing, you lame-brain? I could have helped out earlier. I don't appreciate being dragged around after you as if I didn't matter any more than those two over-dressed wallabies."

Ruth doesn't often get angry and it took me by surprise – though, thinking about it later, I realised it shouldn't have. "You oughtn't to call Australians wallabies," I said, to gain time, "that's racist."

"It's species-ist," said Ruth. "An insult to wallabies."

"They're not so bad," I said cautiously.

"Wallabies are fine," said Ruth, "those two are gruesome – and we both know you only took them on because you thought you might get a chance to boogie with the beach-boy."

"That isn't fair," I said, "I couldn't see how to get rid of them so I rose to the challenge, that's all."

"You thought he was part of the deal, though," said Ruth, "admit it."

"Well, yes, I did, but he wasn't the only reason, honestly. Ruth, please, let's not fall out, I need you."

"You haven't been acting as if you do," said Ruth.

"I'm sorry," I said, and I really was. "I couldn't find a time to tell you – I got caught up in it – I had to keep going and hope for the best."

"Okay, but that's not my fault, is it?" said Ruth. "All this was your idea, right from the start, and I don't know why you invited me along if you weren't going to bother to talk to me. You haven't even let me *eat*!"

Everything she said was horribly true – especially the bit about not eating.

I pointed to a café on the adjoining side of the square, with pavement tables sheltered by the colonnade. "If we sit outside there," I said, "we'll be able to see them come out. We can eat – and I can plan where we take them next. Then we can get shot of them and have a great evening. Okay? Yes?"

"Why can't we just split, right now?" said Ruth. "They're grown up women, they can find their own way back."

I can't pretend I wasn't tempted. The temptation wasn't quite strong enough, though.

"Now that I've taken them on," I said, "I want to make it work. If my father sees I can use my initiative I might get better things to do than tidy brochures."

Ruth flicked her hair about a bit, rattling her beads, but she didn't look seriously angry any more. "I think you should see a doctor about this initiative thing of yours," she said. "Find out if you can't have it surgically removed."

I led the way over to the café, which looked encouragingly nice.

"How long do we get to eat before they finish in there?" said Ruth.

"Not long," I said nervously, "it doesn't look as if it's a very big house." I sat down at the nearest table and slapped the map and the guidebook onto it.

"So what's left of the day's going to be fun, right?" said Ruth, flopping down into the chair opposite and looking at me through narrowed eyes.

"It is," I said. "It definitely is. Trust me! I'm a tour guide!"

CHAPTER NINE

Doubts and Fears

As soon as we sat down at the café table we realised we were desperately thirsty. We ordered mineral waters at once, then Ruth stared at the menu and I stared at the city guide.

"I want everything," said Ruth. "My only problem is where to start. What about you?"

"I'll have what you have," I said, struggling to get the map folded the most useful way.

Ruth glanced up from the menu. "I find that so annoying," she said. "Everyone says women can't fold maps properly – why does Clair have to prove it?"

"Nerves," I said. "M. Deguand said she was a nervous traveller. It's okay, I've got it under control now – and I can remember how to get it back the way she had it if we need to."

"Why would we need to?"

"Because I still think we have to try and track her down. I'm going to have a proper look at the notes she's made in the margin in a minute. But first – quick – I have to create a tour!"

It was amazing how easy it was to work something

out once I could look at the map and guidebook openly. I saw that Place des Vosges, where we were sitting, was at the edge of an area called The Marais. (Words to use when talking to Mrs C and Mrs M: elegant, historic, ancient.) I tried to memorise the fact that the statue of Louis XIII, in the middle of the Place, is only a copy. The real one was melted down in the Revolution. I thought they might like to know that.

"Look," I said to Ruth, "it's obvious. We cross the Square, go out along Rue des Francs Bourgeois, and push them into the Musée de Carnavalet, just to prove we really meant to bring them this way. Then we can weave down through these streets – here – see? – which are bound to be very French and interesting, and work our way to Pont d'Arcole. Cross the bridge and we're on Ile de la Cité, which is where Notre Dame is. Brilliant, eh? Two unexpected things first, then lots of *flânéeing*, and finally the most crucial building in Paris!"

"Sounds like some walk!" said Ruth.

"They can do it," I said. "They're Australians, they're fit. They've got big strong legs, didn't you notice?"

"Hell's teeth!" said Ruth.

"What?"

"They've had enough of Mister Hugo's house. They're marching towards us on their big strong legs right now!"

I swivelled round in my seat. It was horribly true.

I can hardly bear to remember the next bit. Even if I think of it after a huge meal, it still makes me feel hungry. We didn't get to eat a single thing. All we could do was drink down our water, fast, pay for it and move on.

They had not left Victor Hugo's house so soon because they were bored, oh no, they were all charged up with enthusiasm. They'd gone round at high speed in order to get out fast and continue the tour.

"These women have the attention-spans of house-dust mites," Ruth hissed in my ear.

Mrs Mackenzie, to be fair, might have agreed to a short meal-break — but Mrs Cooper announced she had over-eaten at lunchtime and didn't even want to look at food. What was more, she was ready for her next cultural experience. Her personality was so forceful that she swept us off our chairs and pushed us out into the square without so much as touching us. It was all I could do to duck back and shove some francs at the waiter.

You think I was being weedy? Find your own power women and see how you get on!

I marched us across the square to the other side, flinging information over my shoulder as I went, mostly about the wonderfully restored mansions where the aristocracy had lived before the revolution. I also managed to let *them* know that *I* knew that 'Marais' means 'bog or marsh', and that the whole area was built on once-swampy land, reclaimed hundreds of years ago.

"I would especially like to draw your attention," I said, "to Hotel Carnavalet, originally a splendid private house, now a museum, in the once poor street of Francs-Bourgeois – Francs-Bourgeois, of course, meaning 'French Bourgeoisie' or 'the common people'."

"I think hunger's making you light-headed," Ruth growled at my side. "Can we lose them in this museum and get back to the café?"

"There won't be time," I said, once I'd made sure the tour group was too busy oohing and aahing at the architecture to hear me. "They won't be in there long enough. We'd be so tense we wouldn't be able to enjoy it. Listen, we only have to keep this up for about another hour. They must realise tours come to an end sometime. Then we can eat in peace."

"If I don't collapse first," said Ruth. "I bet that airline snack was good."

"We don't eat airline food," I said, with dignity. "We have style. We eat in France. Shall we go into this place with them? It says here it's got the history of Paris and model guillotines and stuff."

"I don't want to spend a second longer with them than I have to," said Ruth, "and I'm keeping my money for food."

"We'll meet you outside," I said as Mrs Cooper overtook us and led the way in. Mrs Mackenzie followed her, an appreciative smile already on her face.

"This is amazing," I said to Ruth, as they disappeared. "They're *really* enjoying themselves. We're *really* giving them a good time."

"Well, whoop-de-do!" said Ruth. "My life has been worthwhile."

I decided to ignore that. We leant together against the outside wall of what was once the most glamorous salon in all Paris and ate four of the fluffy peppermints I found at the bottom of my bag. Then we studied the notes Clair had left in the margin of her map. They were not very informative.

There was a triangle. There was a square with the
bottom line missing. There were the letters ND.
There was something the shape of a lighthouse.
Below that was '15th'. There was a tick by the lighthouse and query marks by the triangle, the broken
square and the ND. Lower down in the margin was
what looked like 'Bld Ste'. And that was it.

"These aren't notes," said Ruth, "they're doodles.
You can't make sense of someone else's doodles.
They might not have anything to do with the trip.
They might be a shopping list for next week, or
memories of childhood traumas, or just patterns she
always draws when she's bored."

"They're all we have to go on," I said.

"I don't see why we have to go on anything,"
said Ruth. "It isn't our business."

"It's why we're *here*, Ruth."

"I know, I know, but we've done all we can and
we can't do any more. Peggy said so. Your father said
so. *I* say so."

I was still looking at the doodles. "There's one bit
here I do understand," I said, "Bld Ste."

"Oh yeah?"

"Bld must be short for Boulevard – and Ste is
short for Sainte, when it's a female saint and has an
'e' on the end. So she must have planned to go
to Boulevard Sainte something. Probably the airline
served her a meal at that moment and she didn't
finish the note."

"Don't talk about meals," said Ruth. She took the
guidebook from me and turned to the list of street
names while I stared blankly at the rest of the
diagrams.

"Okay," said Ruth, after a long pause. "There are twenty-two Sainte-with-an-e street names, but not one of them is a Boulevard."

"Maybe she spelt it wrong, maybe it should have been Saint-without-the-e."

I tried looking at the doodles the other way up but it didn't help. They still looked like a child's first exercise in geometry.

Ruth was standing slumped against the wall, her head bent so far over the guidebook that I couldn't see it for red hair. Eventually she said, "Okay, so there are about 150 Saint-without-an-e-names, and six of them are Boulevards. You can have Denis – " she ran her finger down the list, " – or Germain, or Jacques, or Marcel, or Martin or Michel."

"Are they close to each other?" I said, without much hope.

"Not according to these map references, no. Anyway, suppose we go to each one, what'd we do when we got there? There isn't even a house number. Unless we try number 15."

"It doesn't say 15," I said, "it says 15*th*." Suddenly I remembered something. "I know what 15th means," I said, "it means 15th arondissement – Paris is divided into areas called arondissements."

"Let's see the map," said Ruth, "let's see what's in the 15th."

In the end we crouched down and spread the map on the ground. But though we looked and looked and looked we couldn't find a single Boulevard Sainte Something or even a Boulevard Saint Something in the 15th arondissement.

We heard Mrs Cooper chatting to Mrs Mackenzie

before we saw them – "At least you didn't get lost in there like you did in the Louvre," she was saying.

"Here they come," said Ruth, "so soon! How time flies when you're trying to make sense out of garbage!"

By now, my tour group seemed to have no more doubts about me, and followed willingly when I set off, saying loudly, "I'M GOING TO LEAD YOU TO THE CATHEDRAL OF NOTRE DAME BY A REALLY INTERESTING ROUTE."

As Ruth had said, their attention-spans were short and they were more than willing to do their window-shopping and sightseeing on the trot.

"I've never thought of walking round a city before," said Mrs Cooper. "I always relied on a car. This is a far better idea."

"My feet are beginning to hurt," said Mrs Mackenzie.

"Ignore them," said Mrs Cooper.

I continued my policy of keeping well ahead so I could talk to Ruth. "The ND could stand for Notre Dame, you know," I said.

"Is Notre Dame in the 15th arondy – whatyousaid?"

"No."

"Oh."

We weaved our way through the streets, turning left, then right, then left again, then right again. The tour group found everything as French and appealing as I'd hoped. Even Ruth was looking around her with interest. It became easier and easier to dip in to the guidebook surreptitiously as we walked.

After a while, though I didn't want to spoil things,

I heard myself saying, "I'm beginning to feel uneasy about all this Clair stuff. I'm not sure why, I just am."

"Someone went on a trip with the wrong camera," said Ruth. "Nothing sinister in that."

"Yes, but why didn't she go to the hotel? And why was she so nervous? Look how she's shredded the edges of this map."

"She's a nervous traveller. Jean DeThing said so."

I'd been thinking about that. "But why?" I said. "It's such a short trip and we know she travels a lot. That girl said she books lots of trips through Quest. I can't help thinking she may have been nervous about something else. HERE WE ARE AT RUE DE RIVOLI, WHICH I EXPECT YOU HAVE ALREADY SEEN, SINCE YOUR HOTEL IS NOT FAR AWAY."

We crossed the Rue de Rivoli, not without some difficulty.

"Like what?" said Ruth, eventually, when the sound of French car horns had died back to its usual level.

"Well, that's the trouble, I don't know. And what about M. Deguand, anyway."

"Yes," said Ruth, "*what* about him! Much more appealing than the beach-boy, I'd have said."

"The more I think about him the more I think there was something odd about the way he suddenly appeared like that."

"It was a hotel lobby. Quite a few people suddenly appeared."

"He was so quick to say he'd sat next to Clair."

"Of course. Because he'd overheard we were looking for her."

"Well, why did he say Clair was an unusual name? It isn't."

"Maybe it is in France."

We reached the Place St Gervais exactly as I'd expected and made our way to the riverside.

"THAT'S THE LOUVRE, OVER TO THE RIGHT, BUT WE DON'T GO THERE," I said.

"What's your opinion of the pyramid?" said Mrs Mackenzie.

"Very fine," I said cautiously.

"Yes, I like it," said Mrs Mackenzie.

"Well I find it vulgar and out of place," said Mrs Cooper.

"I wonder what it is," I whispered to Ruth.

"I don't know," said Ruth. "And why are you so suspicious? What's getting to you?"

"Why was M. Deguand so keen to help?"

"He's a nice helpful man. Just because you're devious doesn't mean everyone else is."

"I'm not devious!"

"You are, too! Pretending to know your way round Paris!"

"He was really keen to get hold of that case, Ruth. He offered at once, and then when I couldn't offload it at reception he appeared from nowhere and just spirited it off."

"You didn't tell me that."

"I forgot you didn't know. You'd already gone outside with the others. The hotel wouldn't take responsibility for it so he whisked it off to his room before I could do anything about it."

"If he hadn't, we'd have been schlepping it around with us all afternoon."

"Yes, but why should *he* want to be lumbered with it? WE ARE NOW CROSSING THE SEINE BY PONT D'ARCOLE. Listen – at first I was worried because I thought something might have happened to Clair and I thought that as fellow women we ought to help her. But now . . . what if she's into something illegal?"

"Like what?"

"Well – like smuggling, say?"

Ruth looked at me. "You mean drugs?"

"Perhaps. That would explain why it was so extremely important to bring the right case."

"But the *right* case," said Ruth, staring at me with her eyes extremely wide open, "is the one *we* brought over."

I said, "Exactly." My stomach was doing its washing-machine act again which (I don't know if you've noticed this) is much worse when it's empty. "We may have been really stupid – no, I may have been – it's not your fault. Perhaps the whole thing – that girl rushing in and everything – was part of a plan to get someone else to carry the stuff through for her."

"And you think Mr Deguand may be in on it?" said Ruth.

"Not necessarily – he may be stealing it for his own ends, for all we know."

"Is there *no* possibility, in any scenario you can think of, that Mr Deguand is a genuinely nice man?" said Ruth.

"He could be," I said. "I have no idea what's going on at all, that's what's so awful. But it seems to me highly likely that *either* we've dumped something dubious on a nice, innocent man, *or* that he's involved in something grisly and we ought to tell the police. HERE WE ARE ON ILE DE LA CITÉ – THE VERY OLDEST PART OF PARIS – FIRST INHABITED 2000 YEARS AGO."

"Will you *look* at that Cathedral!" said Mrs Cooper.

"You're getting me worried," said Ruth. "You're making me think we should get back to the hotel."

"I think we should."

"So how do we get rid of those two? Can we dump them in the river, do you think?"

"Almost," I said. "Yes – I think we almost can."

CHAPTER TEN

The Heavy in the Lobby

Ruth swears she didn't really think I was going to shove Mrs C and Mrs M into the Seine. I suppose I believe her – but I definitely remember her clutching my arm and saying "Jo!" with an expression on her face that was halfway between horror and laughter.

"Are you afraid I *am* going to drown them?" I said. "Or are you afraid I'm *not*?"

I raised my voice to the two person tour group and blared, "I DON'T WANT YOU TO GO TO THE CATHEDRAL YET – THERE'S SOMETHING ELSE I'D LIKE YOU TO EXPERIENCE FIRST."

Remembering my guidebook glimpses, I led them to the right, and along beside the Seine towards the square at the far end of Ile de la Cité. I had read that tour boats left from there for one-hour circular cruises – but I didn't announce it at this stage, in case I was wrong.

Then, just as we passed the end of the next bridge to the mainland, Pont Notre Dame, I noticed a tall familiar figure. He was already most of the way across the bridge, walking fast towards us, still looking as though he ought to have a surfboard clamped under one arm. I must have stood still when I saw him, because when I turned to tell the others, I saw they were a good ten metres ahead of me. I opened my mouth to call out to them – and then looked back at the bridge, to make sure I hadn't imagined him.

I hadn't imagined him, and what was more, he'd seen me.

Now don't get me wrong, I wasn't optimistic enough to hope he'd look pleased – but I wasn't ready for him to look totally horrified, either. He stopped abruptly, waved his arms about dramatically, crossing his hands back and forth, then turned sharply and set off back the way he'd come, as fast as he could. Given his long legs and obvious peak condition, that was very fast indeed.

Well, there we go, I thought. As far as Tom is concerned, I have all the appeal of a swarm of malaria-carrying mosquitoes.

I overtook my team, so no one would see that I was having a bit of difficulty with my tear-ducts. Then I got a grip and focused my mind entirely on sending the power women on a river cruise.

I knew I was taking a chance. They might already have done a river trip. The guidebook might be wrong. The last boat of the day might have left. But I'd taken chances all day and they'd all worked out. I was beginning to believe that, as far as tour-guiding went, I was in tune with the universe. I thought I only had to suggest something and it would work. It was a bit like being drunk, I suppose – and probably about as risky.

I got away with it, too.

I walked them to the landing stage, spouting a lot

of stuff about the Seine and how a city built on a river must be seen from the river's-eye-view, and there – waiting – was a boat.

It's true it wasn't due to leave for ten minutes, but it was already taking on passengers, and Mrs Mackenzie was glad of a chance to rest her feet.

Ruth got quite excited. "Terrific!" she said, "I love travelling by water. It's the best thing."

"You can go," I said, and I really meant it. "I have to get back to the hotel and do something about that case before there's some kind of explosion."

"Good grief!" said Ruth. "You think it's a bomb?"

"No, I don't – I mean before the *situation* explodes!"

Ruth's smile faded. "You're right," she said, "we have to get back."

"Not both of us," I said. "You can have a trip."

"Forget it!" said Ruth. "I'd only worry about you."

It was soon obvious that the gruesome twosome didn't expect us to go with them. In fact Mrs Mackenzie said she supposed our jobs must force us to do so much sightseeing in Paris that we must be sick of it.

However, it turned out they did expect us to meet them off the boat afterwards.

"No," said Ruth firmly, looking them each in the eye in turn. "Definitely not. The tour ends here. This is where we say goodbye. Goodbye!"

"I don't think so," said Mrs Cooper, suddenly as tight-lipped and forceful as she'd been at the start. "Your brochure promises a three-hour tour of the city – by the time the boat gets back we shall only have had two and a half."

"My colleague misunderstood," I said, trying to wipe the image of the tall blond retreating figure out of my mind and stay drunk, stay in tune with the universe. "Of course we'll be here to meet the boat."

"I don't *believe* you promised to go back for them," said Ruth, as we jogged towards the hotel. "Have they hypnotised you or what?"

I began to explain that I just wanted to finish what I'd started, but Ruth cut in with, "You're enjoying this, you're actually enjoying it!"

"Okay!" I said. "What would *you* be doing if you weren't here?"

"Chasing after the Munchkins."

"Exactly!"

"Actually," said Ruth, "I don't see a lot of difference. In each case you have a pair of humanoids who are pushy and demanding and don't listen."

"At least these ones don't roll around on the floor and kick."

"It might be more fun if they did. We could sell tickets."

"The major difference is that these two are in Paris! *And* all my gambles are paying off. *And* two power women are doing what *I* tell them!"

"Aha!" said Ruth. "So that's it, is it? You're power-mad! This is a new side to you."

"Power-mad and revolting," I said.

"What?" said Ruth.

So I told her about Tom's reaction when he saw me.

"Come on!" said Ruth. "It was his *aunts* he didn't want to catch up with, not you. He was probably going to take himself on a boat trip and then he saw

79

the golden girls and freaked. Very healthy reaction, I'd say."

"He wiped at the air as if he wanted to erase me," I said gloomily, "and when I think what I look like today, I'm not at all surprised."

"He was signalling to you not to give him away!" said Ruth. "He was putting his trust in you."

"Maybe," I said. "But it looked like rejection from where I was standing."

"Nah," said Ruth, "don't be negative, it was communication."

I was so caught up with thinking this through that we were back at the hotel before we realised we had no idea what to do next.

I pulled Ruth back just as she was about to push through the door into the lobby. "We need a plan," I said. "What have we got so far?"

Ruth counted dramatically on her fingers: "I have aching legs, labouring lungs and an empty stomach," she said. "How about you?"

"I meant – what do we *know*!"

"Nothing," said Ruth, "that's what. We don't know what's going on, we don't know who's doing what, and most of the time we don't even know where we are."

"We know the room number," I said. "Three-two. I remember that's what he said. I think we have to go into that room, get the case and then take it somewhere and have a good look at it."

"Then what?"

"Depends what's in it apart from the camera."

"I know how we get into the room," said Ruth, "I've seen it on the movies a dozen times. We hang around until the maid goes in to change the towels and then we either sneak past her or else we bribe her."

"It's late afternoon," I said. "It's so late, it probably counts as early evening. The rooms will have been done this morning."

"Can we at least go inside the hotel?" said Ruth, looking up at the sky, which was definitely greyer than before. "It could rain."

I said I thought we should make our plans where no one could overhear. "Listen, Ruth, M. Deguand said the case could be collected from him any time. What about simply going to his room and asking for it? We can say we've found Clair. He won't know any different."

"That's fine if he's okay," said Ruth, "but if he's in on something, he's not going to give it to us, is he?"

"Let's face it," I said, "if he *is* in on something, he won't have it with him any more. He went off with it a couple of hours ago – he'll have passed it on by now, if he's going to. So – we go and ask for it and if he gives it to us we know he's honest. Then we just have to check out the case. If he *doesn't* give it to us we get the police and say he stole it."

"Great," said Ruth, "and what if they track it down and find expensive white powder behind a false bottom? Where does that leave us?"

We stood there on the pavement outside the hotel staring at each other for several seconds.

Then Ruth said, "We have to do *something*. Let's do the bit where we go and ask him for it – then we decide the next move after that."

"Right," I said and we strode in.

There was only one other person in the lobby – a big man with hair on the backs of his hands and stubble on his face who was leaning on the counter talking to the perfumed receptionist. As we got there, he finished whatever he was saying but stayed where he was, leaning on the desk and frowning into space.

The receptionist looked at me and raised what was left of her eyebrows. I noticed she'd plucked them to a single hair-line. I explained that I wanted to speak to M. Deguand about Clair Aitken's case.

Reluctantly, she rang through to M. Deguand's room. Then she put down the phone with a flourish, announced he was out, and went back to fiddling with some papers on the desk.

Ruth and I wandered a little way off to consider our next move – and the hairy man followed us. He didn't smile.

"I'm looking for Clair Aitken myself," he said, looming over us. He was even taller than I'd realised, and there were hairs bushing out of his nostrils and ears as well as from the backs of his hands. Ruth said later that he was the nearest thing to a werewolf she'd ever seen.

"I've been hunting around all day," he went on, "and I've been back here about eight times, but it's no use, and this hotel won't take a message. Are you part of the set-up? If I leave word with you will you pass it on?"

I began to tell him that we hadn't been able to find Clair either – and also that it didn't look as if we ever would – but he went on without listening to me.

"The message is that Marco's let us down," he said. "It's a pain but there's nothing I can do. It means it won't be till tomorrow, now."

Ruth started to try to tell him that we had no idea if we could deliver his message or not. He just swatted at the air with one of his huge hands, as if he was brushing her words away, and said, "I'll go on looking, don't you worry, oh yes, I'll go on, I don't give up that easy! But I might as well drop the word wherever I can." He peered at me very closely, "Did I hear you say you've got the camera case?" he said.

"No," I said rapidly, "I haven't got it."

He narrowed his eyes. "I thought you were talking about it," he said, "just now. To Miss Perfume-Bottle-of-the-Year over there."

"That was an entirely different matter," I said, doing my best to sound convincing. "To do with a M. Deguand."

"But you two came over here with Clair, right?"

"We followed on," said Ruth, "but we haven't been able to make contact yet."

"Typical!" said the hairy man. "Well, I'll tell you something you may not know. Clair is accident-prone. Clair is very, very accident-prone indeed. If you ever manage to meet up, say 'Bob says be careful.' Okay? You got all that?"

Without waiting for an answer he turned away and shambled across the lobby.

Ruth and I huddled together and watched as he disappeared into the bar.

"Hell's teeth!" said Ruth. "What was that all about?"

"I have no idea," I said, "but I hated it. What on the planet is Clair mixed up in?"

"Nothing nice," said Ruth. "And what was that about 'accident-prone'? Was that a subtle threat?"

"I thought it was a threat," I said, "but I didn't think it was specially subtle. And who's Marco? The Mafia connection?"

"I owe you an apology," said Ruth. "I thought you were getting worked up about nothing – but now I don't."

I was trying to run through the recent conversation in my head. "I hope I didn't give too much away," I said at last.

"How could you?" said Ruth. "We don't know anything. We have to get that case, we have to snitch the key and go get it." She began to move very slowly towards the door into the bar.

"Where are you going?" I hissed at her.

"Just want to make sure Godzilla's well settled in there with a blood-cocktail, or whatever he drinks," Ruth hissed back. "Don't want him coming out and interrupting." She sidled up to the door, glanced in, and then shot back to my side like a bullet. "Yup, he's deep in the bar," she said, "but guess who's sitting in there, too, with his back to the door?"

"M. Deguand?"

"Himself" said Ruth. "So do we ask him for the case?"

"What!" I said. "With the Hairy Hulk in there? I think *not*. But if you look back at the desk you'll see our fragrant friend is on the phone with her back to the key-rack. Let's do what you said – let's pinch the key."

"It won't be there," said Ruth, "he'll have it with him in the bar."

"Well, we can look," I said. "You look, and I'll watch her. If she comes off the phone I can keep her attention away from you. I can speak to her in French – that seems to infuriate her."

"Okay," said Ruth, "so what number am I looking for?"

"Thirty two."

It was almost too easy to get the key. The receptionist didn't so much as glance round and no one else came into the lobby. Ruth hung over the far end of the counter till her feet were off the floor, unhooked Key 32, and turned at once towards the lift. I caught at her arm and pointed to the staircase. I was afraid the sound of the lift might draw attention to us.

"It'll be the third floor," I said as we ran up the stairs on tiptoe. "That's usually how they mark keys – floor number first, then room number."

"I may be too weak to climb that high," said Ruth, but she managed it, and almost too soon we were standing in a short narrow corridor outside a door with 32 written on it.

Ruth pointed the key towards the keyhole – and then hesitated.

"Go on," I said. "We know he's not in there, we know he's in the bar."

Ruth put the key into the keyhole – but she still hesitated.

"Hurry up," I said. "We're only going to take back something he should never have had in the first place. We're not doing anything wrong."

"I hope your French is good enough to explain that to the Paris police," said Ruth, turning the key and gently pushing the door open.

"It won't come to that," I said, pushing it wider, "we won't get caught."

CHAPTER ELEVEN

Entering Without Breaking

We closed the door behind us and looked carefully around Room 32. Apart from a large empty carry-all, folded up on the stool at the end of the bed, and a hairbrush and comb on the dressing table, there was no sign that anyone was staying there at all.

"How can such a stylishly scruffy man be so obsessively tidy in his room?" said Ruth. "It's so tidy it's frightening. I daren't move."

"Don't worry," I said, "we won't need to ransack it. If the case is here it'll be easy to find."

Ruth walked over to a door in the corner of the room and stared at it for a moment. Then she opened it, looked in, said, "Just what I wanted," and disappeared through it, shutting it behind her.

"What have you found?" I said stupidly, half believing it was the camera case.

"Guess," said Ruth, her voice muffled by the door and echoing a bit. Then I heard the sound of the flush.

Ruth reappeared saying, "Does Paris have public bathrooms?"

"Not really. Just those stand-up things for men, in the middle of the street."

"That's what I figured," said Ruth, holding the door for me. "Go for it while you can."

The bathroom was as tidy as the bedroom had been. There was just one toothbrush, in the mug provided, and a zippered shaving kit. The case was definitely not in there, not even behind the shower-curtain.

When I came out, we began on the bedroom.

"I've been thinking about those doodles on the map," said Ruth, as we looked in each of the double wardrobes in turn.

I dragged a straight-backed chair over and stood on it to look in the cupboards above the wardrobes. They were full of spare bedding.

"You know you thought ND could be Notre Dame?" Ruth went on.

I began to hand down spare pillows and blankets to her, in the vague hope the case might have been hidden behind them. It hadn't.

"Well, remember our two favourite Australians?" said Ruth, as she handed the pillows and blankets back up to me. "Remember they talked about a pyramid at the Louvre? Well, a diagram of a pyramid would look like a triangle, right?"

I climbed down from the chair and put it back where I'd got it.

Then I went to the room door and listened. There was no sound of anyone in the corridor – and I thought we'd have heard if someone had used the lift.

I crossed to the bed and lay down on the floor to look underneath it.

"Say ND *is* Notre Dame," Ruth persisted, "and say the triangle *is* a pyramid at the Louvre, then the others will be famous sights as well. Are you listening to me?"

There was nothing whatsoever under the bed. I stood up.

"*Must* we try and work this out while we're trespassing in a strange Frenchman's room?" I said. "I can't concentrate."

"I can," said Ruth. "Fear has sharpened my mind. That square with the bottom line missing, remember? That could be an arch. Isn't there some famous arch in Paris?"

"The Arc de Triomphe," I said. "You might be right. So what's the thing that looks a bit like a lighthouse? That's the one she ticked."

We both got it at the same time.

"The Eiffel Tower!" we said – and then stopped, our hands over our mouths, shaken at the noise we'd made.

"Let's get out of here," said Ruth, "there's nowhere else he could possibly have put a case as big as that one. He must have passed it on to someone."

I looked round the room one more time. Ruth was right, there were no hiding places left.

"Right, let's go," I said. I opened the door to the corridor – and found myself nose to nose with an old man who was standing immediately outside it.

We both gasped and stepped back. He recovered first.

"What are you doing in my room!" he said. He

spoke in English because he was English. Then he began to repeat the question in bad French, but I interrupted him. I knew I had to talk us out of this instantly, or not at all.

"I *do* beg your pardon," I said, "we must have picked up the wrong key at reception – and you know how it is – all hotel rooms look alike – so it was a few seconds before we realised our mistake."

I was pushing out past him as I spoke.

Ruth followed me, struggling with various expressions, including guilt, panic and smiling apology.

"This is *so* embarrassing," I said, "thank goodness you weren't in there when we walked in. This must be yours."

I held the key out to him and he took it from me. He seemed to have his anger on hold.

"I got all the way up here," he said, "before I realised I hadn't collected my key, and then the door just *opened* . . ."

Ruth had decided which expression to go for. It was the one that made the most of her large blue eyes. "I just hope you weren't as frightened as we were," she said. "We had no idea you were outside the door – and of course you had no idea we were inside it!"

My efforts had left him looking a bit dazed. Faced with Ruth, he began to melt.

"Not to worry," he said, "it's easily done . . ."

"Thank you for being *so* understanding," said Ruth, giving him the full force of her best smile.

Melt-down was complete.

"*I* should thank *you*," he said, "you've saved me

going all the way back down again. But now of course you have to go back down for your key."

"That's our punishment for making such a stupid mistake," gushed Ruth.

He stood watching us as we walked away. Ruth looked back and waved as we turned the corner of the corridor.

"Do you think he was suspicious?" she whispered to me, as we started down the stairs.

"No," I said, "just infatuated."

"Oh, *please*! He must be at least seventy!"

"They're never too old to dream," I said. "That could have been really nasty, you know. Maybe I'm not in tune with the universe any more."

"Good grief," said Ruth. "I didn't know you thought you were. That's *really* scary."

"Listen," I said, "I think I've worked it out – I think I know how I got the room number wrong."

"Better late than never, I guess," said Ruth. "How?"

"I thought he said 'three um two' . . . I assumed he was struggling to remember. But maybe he said 'three on two' – meaning room three on floor two. In which case he's in twenty three – not thirty two."

"So are you telling me we have to go steal another key?"

"If it's there. I think you may be right, I think he may have it with him as he's only in the bar."

Ruth stopped at the corner of the last flight. "We'd better go carefully," she said. "We don't want that receptionist to see us coming down the stairs. She'd be certain to ask what we're doing."

"I've just thought of something else," I said. "Clair Aitken is a professional photographer."

"So?"

"So – she's not going to travel to Paris and take pictures of Notre Dame and the Eiffel Tower, is she? There must be a million pictures of those places, taken from every possible angle, at every possible hour of the day or night. She'd be looking for unusual things – unexpected things."

"I hate to admit it, but you're right," said Ruth. "So those *were* just doodles?"

"I think they probably were," I said, sidling cautiously down the last few stairs and peering round the corner into the lobby. The last thing I felt I needed at that moment was another shock. But I got one anyway.

It was all right at first. The receptionist was on the telephone – either still or again. I signed to Ruth to come on down and we walked slowly and quietly across the lobby towards the street door. I hoped that if she looked round, she'd think we'd just come out of the bar. Which was why I began to relax as we got level with the bar door.

And at that moment M. Deguand came out, accompanied by one of the most beautiful and elegant women I've ever seen in my life, as smooth as he was shaggy.

"Ah, hallo again," he said, looking quite pleased to see us, "I have just been telling my wife about your problems. I trust your conducted tour in the company of the two ladies was a success?"

I smiled weakly. "Yes, thank you," I said, "it went very well."

"Good, excellent," said M. Deguand, and his wife produced the kind of dazzling smile that not even Ruth could have achieved.

I was so surprised, I let them get almost all the way to the lift before I reacted. "M. Deguand," I said, realising positive action was needed. "That camera case you're so kindly looking after for us . . ."

M. Deguand pressed the button for the second floor. Then he turned back, smiled charmingly, pushed his hand through his shaggy hair and said, "Ah yes, of course, I do beg your pardon, I should have told you. I have returned the camera case."

"What?" said Ruth.

"Yes, to Clair's other friend," said M. Deguand. "I encountered him in the bar a few moments ago. He explained that he had already spoken with you. So he has taken it now and all is well."

He pulled the lift doors open and he and Madame disappeared into it.

"This is a nightmare!" said Ruth. "He's given the case to Godzilla."

We moved as one to look into the bar – but it was empty. We hurried out of the hotel – but there was no sign of a large hairy man anywhere, in either direction or on either side of the street.

"I can't find the client," I said, "and now I don't know where the case is. Have I got any credibility left?"

"You know that myth about you losing things?" said Ruth. "Well, I'm beginning to understand how it started."

CHAPTER TWELVE

And the Number You Need is . . .

We set off to meet Mrs Cooper and Mrs Mackenzie in a state of deep gloom. After a while I said I thought this might be partly because our blood sugar level was a bit low.

"A *bit* low?" said Ruth. "Mine's round my ankles."

I tried to reassure her that the end of the tour was in sight. "We meet them off the boat, lead them to Notre Dame and let them get on with it," I said.

"I hope that'll leave us time to eat before we have to head back to the airport," said Ruth.

I said I didn't know if I'd have any appetite now everything had turned nasty.

Ruth just muttered something about an emergency and turned in at the door of a *tabac*.

I'd failed Ruth so totally that I was beginning to wonder if I'd damaged our friendship forever. "This isn't how I expected the day to turn out," I said feebly, as I followed her in.

Ruth didn't answer.

I watched as she bought a Snickers bar. "Everything all right now?" I said hopefully, as she ripped off the wrapper.

"We are in France," said Ruth, "famous home of delicious cuisine, and I am eating an American candy bar. Does that sound all right to you?"

"We could buy postcards while we're in here," I said, hoping to jolly her along. "We don't have to post them, we can just show them around when we get back. That'd be good, wouldn't it?"

"No," said Ruth, with her mouth full.

"Well, if we're not going to buy anything else, why aren't we leaving?"

"I have to eat this right here," said Ruth. "In case I need another one."

"All right," I said brightly, "let's choose souvenirs while you finish it."

It was a very small *tabac* with a very small souvenir shelf, mostly stacked with models of the Eiffel Tower and French poodle fridge magnets. Somehow, I couldn't work up much excitement about buying any of them.

"Nah," said Ruth. She finished the Snickers, put the wrapper in her pocket, and went back to the counter for a packet of sugared almonds.

"Nothing for Gareth?" I said, still hoping to get her back into some kind of holiday mood.

"Nah," said Ruth again. Then, "Oh, wait – yes – I should get something for George."

"George!" I said, as a vivid picture of George in the Quest Travel shop floated in front of my mind. "George!"

"Yes," said Ruth, "you know, George. Short guy, closely related to me."

I couldn't believe I hadn't thought of George before, and I said so.

"You want to buy him something, too?" said Ruth, nudging me out of the shop. "Okay, but not in there, it's garbage. Not that George doesn't respond well to garbage, because he does, but not that kind of garbage."

"No, listen," I said, as Ruth strode off along the pavement. "George sold raffle tickets to Clair's assistant when she brought in the camera case. She bought a whole bookful of them."

"So?"

"So she'll have put her name and address on the stubs."

"So?"

"So we can ring George and get him to look her up in the phone book. And don't say 'so?' again."

"Am I allowed to say 'How will that help?' "

"It will help because it will mean we can probably get hold of her. Dad couldn't get her at the studio, but we're quite likely to be able to get her at home. We can find out if she knows where Clair planned to go. We can ask what to do about the case."

"You mean the case we haven't got any more?" said Ruth acidly. "You mean *that* case?"

"Oh. Just for a second I'd forgotten."

"I think we'd be wise to forget the whole thing," said Ruth. "You said yourself – *she* might be in on the smuggling, or whatever."

"Ruth, we don't even know that there's *been* any smuggling, or whatever. We just know Clair's missing. And the only other person who knows she's missing is that menacing man in the lobby, issuing threats. We can ask that girl if she knows anyone called – what did he say his name was?"

"Bob, I think."

"Bob – or anyone called Marco."

Ruth heaved an enormous sigh. "I thought your obsession with Clair was over," she said. "I thought I only had to cope with your obsession with the Sydney belles."

"We've got nearly fifteen minutes till the boat gets back," I said. "Let's find a phone as near as we can to the landing place. Yes? Ruth, you agree? How are we going to feel if we do nothing and ages later we hear something awful happened to her. Come on, what happened to sisterhood?"

"Oh brother!" said Ruth. "Okay, chill out, I'm with you. I'll call George at Danny's and just hope he's got the ticket stubs with him."

George had got the ticket stubs with him at Danny's, which was good news. George also had Danny with him, which was not such good news. I've always thought of George as really sensible, but then I always see him when he's with Ruth and trying to live up to her. Danny brings out something quite different in him. Something you'd like to exterminate.

First of all he told Ruth he didn't know exactly where the stubs were and that he'd have to search. It isn't all that easy to hear when you're sharing the receiver of a public telephone near a busy Parisian tourist spot, but the search sound effects George and Danny created came over loud and clear.

"Come *on*, George," said Ruth, as the rustling and scrabbling and sniggering poured down the wires.

"Come *on*, come *on*," she said, as the sound of

drawers opening and shutting, doors slamming and the hamster spinning in its wheel, followed.

"I'd like to kill whoever invented the portable phone," she said, as windows slid up and down, the garden gate swung squeakily, and the automatic garage doors cranked into action.

At last George decided to be merciful and admit he had the stubs in his hand. "Her name *is* on them," he said. "It's Tricia."

"Is there an address!" said Ruth.

"Why? Are you going to write to her?" said George.

"No," said Ruth, through gritted teeth, "I'm going to ask you to look her up in the phone book."

"Oh, you want me to look her up in the phone book," said George and we could hear Danny snorting and drumming his heels.

"George!" said Ruth. "You're talking yourself out of a present from Paris."

"I'd like to tell you her address," said George, "but I can't."

"Why not?"

"She didn't write it down."

"Maybe she's got an unusual surname," I said, "maybe you can still find her in the book."

"She didn't put her surname, either," said George. Danny was laughing so much he sounded as if he was going to be sick.

"Danny," yelled Ruth. "*Nothing's* that funny!"

"Let's not waste any more money on this call," I said. "It was a good idea that failed."

"Bye, George," said Ruth.

"Don't you want me to tell you her phone

number?" said George. "She's written it right here, just after her name."

Ruth doesn't usually get cross with George and I think he was quite surprised at her reaction, which was loud and went on for quite a long time. I was less surprised. But then George didn't know the kind of day she was having and I did.

The way our luck had been going, we weren't surprised at all to find that Tricia was out when we rang. Tricia's mother was in, though, and she was able to tell us something.

"I'm afraid Tricia's gone off for the day," she said, "and I don't know where, so I can't get in touch. All I can tell you is that Clair's in Paris on a fashion shoot. I think it's for some catalogue of city suits. I am *so* sorry that Tricia caused all this bother by putting out the wrong case!"

We didn't tell her we had no idea where the case was. We just asked if she'd ever heard Tricia mention someone called Bob – or Marco.

"No," she said, "I'm sorry."

Then we asked if she knew where Clair might be.

"I'm afraid I don't," she said. "Out on location, I suppose."

We thanked her and hung up.

"Are you thinking what I'm thinking?" I said to Ruth, as we walked on down to the landing stage where the Seine boat was just tying up.

"Try me."

"Well, a photographer doesn't do a fashion shoot alone, does she?"

"Nope," said Ruth, "there'd be a team."

"And I don't expect there's a law that says you can't

be on a fashion shoot team just because you have
hairy hands and tufty ears."

"True," said Ruth. "I feel bad about Godzilla – I
think we did him an injustice – I think he's possibly
genuinely hunting for Clair, with a genuine message."

The gangway was pushed into position and the
passengers began to make their way off. At first there
was no sign of Mrs C and Mrs M.

"And when he said 'we can't do it today'," I said,
"he wasn't talking about a drugs drop, he was talking
about the shoot. And – of course – Marco – the one
who's let them down . . ."

". . . is probably the model," nodded Ruth.

"So why was he so menacing?"

"I don't think he really was," said Ruth. "I think
he was just tense – and maybe a bit short on charm."

"What about 'tell Clair to be careful', then and
'Clair is accident prone'?"

I had now spotted Mrs Cooper and Mrs Mackenzie in the midst of the crowd and they had spotted
us. They began to head our way.

"Statement of fact, maybe," said Ruth. "And probably accurate, if you think about it."

"So Jean Deguand really was just being helpful.
He really is a nice man."

"Shame about his wife," said Ruth.

"She seemed nice, too."

"You know what I mean!" said Ruth.

"Something else," I said. "Now we know what the
pictures are for, we can forget about arty shots of
unknown corners of the city. The only point in
coming to Paris to take pictures for a catalogue would

be to show the places that everyone on the planet can recognise."

"The Eiffel Tower's the one she ticked," said Ruth.

"Could you bear it . . .?"

"To be truthful," said Ruth, as our two charges loomed ever closer, "I'd quite like to see it myself. I know it's corny, but it *is* Paris, isn't it. Only snag is – she won't be there. However dopey she is, she'll have noticed several hours ago that no one else has shown."

"I know I've said this before – but it's all we have to go on."

"It doesn't matter now, anyway," said Ruth. "God-zilla-the-Good's on her trail, with her case. It's out of our hands in every way."

"We don't *know* he's a good guy," I said, "and anyway he doesn't know about the Eiffel Tower connection."

"Let's do a deal," said Ruth. "We go to the E.T. because we want to anyway. Then when we find she's not there, we give up on her. Finally. Totally. Completely."

I didn't have to think about it for very long. "That makes sense," I said.

Ruth lowered her voice as Mrs C and Mrs M bore down on us. "Point them at Notre Dame and let's go," she said.

Mrs Cooper was already talking as she stomped up to us. "That was an excellent trip," she said, speaking rather sternly and not smiling.

"It's been a lovely afternoon altogether," said Mrs Mackenzie, but she wasn't smiling either, and she glanced almost nervously at Mrs Cooper as she spoke.

"Now then," said Mrs Cooper, who was clearly back in full power mode, "while we waited for the boat to start we found we had time to read through our travel literature more carefully. We have discovered that we are not booked on a guided tour of Paris – there is no mention of any guides or couriers in Paris at all. Who *are* you?"

CHAPTER THIRTEEN

The Site in Question

The rest of the boatload wandered off to enjoy itself, but not us. We stood still, trapped by two indignant Australians. They waited – not especially patiently – for our explanation.

My first instinct was to tell them the truth. Apart from anything else, I've found it usually saves a lot of bother. I should have known better, though. After all, it didn't work the first time I tried it, so why should it work now?

"I did tell you," I said, "that you weren't booked on a tour of Paris."

"Nonsense!" said Mrs Cooper. "I remember exactly what you said – you said, 'We'll take you on our Essential Paris Trip'!" She turned to Mrs Mackenzie. "Am I right?" she said.

"Absolutely," said Mrs Mackenzie. "And very good it was, too."

"That's irrelevant," said Mrs Cooper sharply. She turned back to us. "Do you have some identification?" she said. Then, when we hesitated, "Come along, come along."

I remembered Ruth saying earlier, 'Have they

hypnotised you or what?' and I thought that maybe Mrs C had, in a way. Why else did I find it impossible not to do as she told me.

Obediently I took my passport out of my bag. Meekly I showed it to her.

Ruth shrugged and fished out her own passport, but she offered it in an entirely different way, flicking it open in an excellent imitation of a TV cop showing his ID to a low-life.

Mrs Cooper was not impressed. "These give us your names," she said, "I see no proof of any connection with Quest Travel."

"I do work for Quest," I said, with all the dignity I could manage, "but as I explained in the hotel, I am not your courier."

"Then why," said Mrs Cooper, bristling with hostility, "did you first of all say, 'We'll take you on our Essential Paris Trip' and *then* say, 'We leave immediately'? I have a very good memory, you know, and so does Mrs Mackenzie."

"Yes, I do remember you saying that," said Mrs Mackenzie. "Quite definitely."

"We put ourselves in your hands," said Mrs Cooper. "It seems you abused our trust."

"I think," said Ruth, loudly, brightly, positively, "that perhaps we didn't explain too clearly back at the hotel. We got side-tracked fixing your room changes, *if* you remember. Essential Paris is a brand new tour and today was a trial offer, completely free of charge. We are very happy that you chose to take it. We hope you had a nice day."

So that's what you do with power women, I

thought, as they stood quietly digesting her words, you power right back at them.

"Where were you going to take us next?" asked Mrs Cooper, after a few seconds.

Ruth and I answered simultaneously.

"Notre Dame," said Ruth, pointing in one direction.

"The Eiffel Tower," said I, pointing in the other.

"There seems to be some confusion," said Mrs Mackenzie.

"We were going to give you the option," said Ruth rapidly, shooting me a ferocious look. "But Notre Dame is by far the more interesting."

"We're quite tired," said Mrs Cooper. I could see that her indignation had gone, but I couldn't tell what mood it had left her in. "We had a flight this morning, don't forget. ("Tell me about it," muttered Ruth.) And the weather doesn't look good. I think we'd prefer to go back to our hotel now. Where can I get a taxi?"

"There's a rank just across the bridge," I said, "at Place de L'École, but it's hardly worth it. Once you're there it's only a few minutes walk to the hotel."

"We shall get a taxi," said Mrs Cooper firmly. Then, quite unexpectedly, she stuck out her hand. "Quest Travel will be hearing from us," she said.

Solemnly, we all shook hands, then she and Mrs M set off to cross Pont Neuf to the right bank.

"Heaven knows what they'll say to Dad," I said to Ruth. "But thanks. You saved me again."

"Think nothing of it," said Ruth. "I'm a traditionalist. I know the U.S. Cavalry always rides to the rescue. Shame it's the horse's day off."

"We need to cross the other way," I said, "to the left bank, if we want to get the Metro to the Eiffel Tower."

"Before we do," said Ruth, clutching my arm and pointing, "don't you want to say 'Hi' to a friend?"

I guessed who I was going to see even before I turned round. Tom, walking slowly towards us, but not looking at us, looking at the back view of his aunts as they disappeared in search of their cab.

"Have they gone," he said as he reached us, "or are they about to come back?"

"They've had it for the day," said Ruth, "they're headed for their hotel and a sleep before dinner."

"They're fine, really," said Tom, "I'm fond of 'em, but I just prefer to cruise around on my own." He gave me a dazzling smile. "Hey, thanks for not giving me away," he said.

"That's okay."

"I know it's corny," said Tom, "but I really want to do the boat trip. Are they still running, do you know?"

"One's loading now," said Ruth, "I can see it from here."

"So what are you guys up to?" said Tom. "Do you feel like hanging out together tomorrow?"

I was too stunned to answer, but Ruth said, "That would've been good, but we fly back tonight."

"Too bad," said Tom. "Well, maybe I'll catch you in London instead?"

"You're coming back to London?" I bleated.

"S'right." He counted on his fingers. "We do Florence, Rome and Vienna. Then we would've flown home from there, but we have an Aged Relly

106

in England. The Aunts are going to scoop him up and carry him back to end his days in Oz. So we have to go back at the end."

"That's great!" said Ruth.

"You could show me round," said Tom, and, as Ruth kept reminding me later, he looked directly at me as he said it. "You're the first person I've ever met who wasn't frightened of the Aunts."

"How do you know I wasn't?" was all I could think of to say.

"You didn't show it, anyway," said Tom. "That'll do. Will I find you if I call in at the Travel Agency – what's it called – Quest?"

"She'll be there," said Ruth, after waiting a few seconds to see if I was going to manage to answer him.

"I'll be there," I said, pulling myself together, "and I'll be a bit better dressed next time."

"Oh no, don't be," said Tom, "I can't stand it when chicks are all dished up, makes me nervous."

I couldn't imagine him nervous, but I definitely was. I think we all talked some more but I can't remember what about. Then Tom said, "Hey, it looks as if the boat's ready for off. See you!"

"See you in London," I said, as he took off towards the quay at speed.

"Cool!" said Tom, his voice drifting back over his shoulder.

"Look at him run!" said Ruth dreamily. Then she turned back to me. "Brilliant!" she said. "You have a date!"

"If he wanted a date," I said, "he could have asked us to go on the boat trip with him, now."

"That would've been both of us," said Ruth. "In London he can just get you."

"Maybe," I said, "Maybe it was you he liked."

"Why do you always *do* that?" said Ruth. "It was you, of course it was you."

"By the time he's back in London," I said, "he'll have forgotten."

"I give up," said Ruth. "Lead me to the Tower!"

We made our way to the Metro Station at Quai St Michel and caught the RER a couple of stops over to the Eiffel Tower.

"I can see why Tom likes sightseeing without them," I said. "It's so peaceful."

"You nearly brought them along," said Ruth.

"I know – I got in a muddle."

"I was beginning to think they'd be with me for the rest of my life."

"You know Mrs Cooper said Quest would hear from her again – was that a threat or a promise, do you think?"

"No idea," said Ruth. "They've gone, they're over, they're done with – I don't even want to *think* about them ever again. Their nephew can be mentioned, as often as you like, but keep quiet about those women, will you?"

The Tower, when we got to it, was a surprise – much bigger than either of us had expected, and much more impressive. It was just as well, because it was the single bit of normal sightseeing we did that day – and it didn't last long.

"It's brown," said Ruth.

"What did you expect?" I said, craning my neck

to watch a lift creeping up one of the huge legs. "Green plastic?"

"I think I thought it was black," said Ruth. "And smaller. Definitely smaller." She turned slowly, staring upwards. "It's beautiful," she said.

"No sign of a fashion shoot," I said, looking around at the milling tourists. "But there's a shop over there, in one of the legs – shall I ask if they've seen anyone with a camera?"

"Are you serious?" said Ruth.

For a second I didn't know what she meant – then I began to giggle.

"They will have seen a *thousand* people with cameras," said Ruth, "and that's just in the last half hour."

"I know," I said, "I'm off my head. And like you said, she wouldn't still be here anyway. Forget her – let's enjoy this."

At that moment I really believed I'd pushed Clair Aitken out of my head, along with Mrs Cooper and Mrs Mackenzie, forever.

"So do we go up it?" said Ruth, walking about underneath it with her head tipped back. "What do you think?"

I looked at my watch. "Well . . ." I said.

Ruth looked at her own watch. "Right," she said, "we have a plane to catch. I guess it's a choice between riding up or eating, yes?"

"Yes."

"Next time we come to Paris we go up," said Ruth. "Now, we eat. Any ideas?"

I'd already had a look at the Eiffel Tower area in the guidebook while we were on the train. "There is somewhere that doesn't seem too far away," I said. "It's a bit of a walk, but it looks as if it should be good, and it's cheap."

"Lead on," said Ruth, sounding quite bouncy. We hadn't walked far, though, when her spirits began to go downhill again rather sharply. A mixture of tiredness, hunger and the fact that the gathering clouds had decided to empty themselves on our heads, I suppose.

"Where *is* this place?" she said.

"In this direction, I promise."

"Are you sure you know exactly where you're taking me? I don't entirely trust you – you won't be surprised to hear."

I held out the map to her as we walked. "See," I said, "we're here and we just have to get there."

"And you're sure they'll be open and cooking when we get there?" said Ruth, without bothering to look at it.

"Yes. What's the matter with you? You're from pioneering stock, you should be more adventurous."

"I'm adventurous, I'm *very* adventurous. I'll try out a new perfume any time someone gives me one. I just don't appreciate being lost in a strange city in the rain."

"Listen, pioneering was never comfortable. According to that school project you did, your lot went out with some of the earliest settlers. Adventuring must be in your genes – and don't make any feeble jokes."

"My genes got all that out of their system several generations back," said Ruth. "Right now they like to live easy."

"There's nothing very tough about walking to a restaurant."

"It's raining."

"But it's romantic rain – it's French rain – *Il pleut*!"

"I'm sorry," said Ruth, "I don't mean to be rude, but I don't see what's romantic about walking along a French sidewalk with you while *pleut* runs into my eyes."

"You don't say sidewalk – you're anglicised – you say pavement."

"In France I say sidewalk, okay? Don't hassle me. I'm nervous, I'm trying to hang on to my identity."

"I know what your trouble is, the Snickers bar has worn off."

"They're not meant to keep you going forever."

"I was thinking about the Eiffel Tower," I said, deciding it was time to change the subject, "and about how big it is."

"Sure is," said Ruth.

"And I was thinking – the one place you couldn't photograph it from is *at* it. You'd never get it all in the shot."

"A person equipped with a professional camera and a wide-angle lens could do what she liked," said Ruth. "Assuming we're talking about the invisible but somehow ever-present Ms Aitken."

"No. Think about it. Think about a fashion shoot. The model would have to appear big enough for the clothes to be seen. If you had a model filling the frame *at* the Eiffel Tower, you'd be lucky to get part of one of the tower legs in shot."

Ruth plodded on without comment.

"You'd want the Tower in the background," I said

casually, "so you'd go some way off – probably into the next arondissement. The Tower's right at the edge of the 7th, but because the numbers spiral outwards, the next one's the 15th."

Ruth kept walking, and didn't look at me, but she said, "A horrible thought has just occurred to me. Where are we? Which arondissement just happens to contain this restaurant we're headed for?"

"The 15th, actually."

"I *knew* it. You *haven't* given up on her!"

"If you look at this map," I said, "you'll see that two people wanting to eat cheaply, and starting off on foot from the Eiffel Tower, would be likely to head into the 15th."

"Maybe," said Ruth, still not looking at it.

I was quite certain that I knew where I was taking us, but even so, I was very relieved when, quite soon, I saw the restaurant sign, just one block ahead of us. "There!" I said, pointing and nudging Ruth.

"Right!" said Ruth. Her head came up, her smile came back, and she began to walk faster, her eyes fixed on the restaurant front.

That's why she didn't notice anything else in the street.

We reached the restaurant and Ruth stopped at the menu board outside, wiped the raindrops off it with a wet hand, and began to read. "I don't understand a word of this, but it looks absolutely brilliant," she said.

I stood beside her, trying to pay attention to what was on offer, but with most of my mind on the large building opposite. Its ground floor was complete, but above that there seemed to be not much more than a towering scaffolding structure, with a few isolated bits of second-floor wall.

"Look!" I said to Ruth, tugging her damp sleeve and pointing.

Ruth glanced round briefly. "That'll be nice when it's finished," she said, "but it doesn't serve food so I'm not interested."

"Ruth," I said, wanting her to think of it first, to reassure me I wasn't completely mad. "What is it?"

"What do you mean 'what is it?' It's a partly built building."

"But what *is* it?"

"It isn't anything yet. What's the matter with you? It's a building site, okay?"

"And if you were doodling in the margin of a map," I said, "making an abbreviated note for yourself, what would you write down?"

Ruth turned away from the menu very slowly. There was a moment, I knew, when she almost decided to ignore me and turn back to it. Then she said, "Show me the map again."

We both looked at it. Near the rough outline that we had decided was the Eiffel Tower was scribbled '15th' and then 'Bld Ste'.

"I see what you're thinking," said Ruth. "She was going to a building site in the 15th which had a good view of the Eiffel Tower. Only snag is – look around – you can't see the Eiffel Tower from here."

"Perhaps you can from the other side," I said. "I tell you what – you go in and get a table and order – and I'll just take a quick look."

"No," said Ruth, and she heaved the hugest sigh

I'd ever heard. "I won't be able to relax – I'll only worry that you're out here using your initiative. We'll go together. But for pity's sake let's make it fast."

CHAPTER FOURTEEN

Out of the Depths

"No," I said to Ruth firmly, trying to power at her the way she'd powered at the power women. "Get into that restaurant and order. It's almost seven – we have to head for the airport by eight. Your dinner is endangered – get in there and save it."

"How about *your* dinner?" said Ruth. "Or have you given up eating entirely?"

"I'll join you, I told you. But I have to go and look first."

"What if I get in there and start eating and you don't show?" said Ruth. "At what point do I decide to fling down my fork and come look for you? Even *my* appetite can't override that kind of anxiety. Can't we get a later flight?"

"It'd cost money to switch – and what if there are no seats and we have to stay over?"

"I can think of worse places to be stuck in."

"We'd have to charge the hotel to Dad. He'd pay – but he would *not* be a happy parent."

"Come on then," said Ruth, glancing rapidly in both directions and accidentally flicking me in the face with a mixture of hair and beads. "It's clear," and she lit off across the street so fast she was at the corner before I'd caught her up.

I don't suppose I'd ever looked at a half-built building so carefully before. Probably they all look strange. That one certainly did. It was fenced in by the usual kind of hoardings, but in places the huge boards had partly fallen sideways so you could see through to the ground floor. The shell of the ground floor looked finished, but none of the detailing was there. There were door-frames but no doors, window-frames but no windows.

The first floor was easier to see in one way – because the hoardings didn't reach up that far. At the same time it was harder, because it was higher.

On the side that faced the restaurant, the first floor had mostly been scaffolding. On the far side, when we reached it, the scaffolding stopped, because on that side the first floor was more or less finished. Again, without doors in the doorways or windows in the window holes.

Enormous sheets of green tarpaulin and bright blue plastic overlapped each other on top of the whole thing, more or less protecting the open bits from the rain, except where they'd slipped.

In at least two places on the sagging hoardings there was a picture of the head and shoulders of an Alsatian, showing its teeth.

"That's nice," said Ruth, "they have guard dogs. What's 'sit' in French?"

"*Asseyez-vous.*"

"Too long, what's 'help'?"

"*Au secours.*"

116

"Nearly as bad. No problem, I'll just scream and run."

"There may not be any dogs there," I said. "They may just be hoping the pictures'll put people off."

"In my case," said Ruth, "they could get lucky."

"It would be possible to go in, now we're round this side," I said – a bit doubtfully, I have to admit.

It was true that the sag in the hoardings seemed to offer a reasonably wide entrance. It was also true that the building, or what there was of it, looked very much less than welcoming.

"Have you looked behind you?" said Ruth.

I turned round. There, before my eyes, was a magnificent view of the Eiffel Tower – distant enough to look romantic, close enough to be seen clearly.

"Oh. Look at that!" I said.

"I am looking at it," said Ruth.

"Think how that would look from one of those," I said, pointing at the enormous, glassless, first floor windows. "The designer of the shoot could probably arrange to get a desk and chair up there – model-Marco could sit casually on the edge of the desk, city suit perfectly pressed, picture window behind him framing the Tower. No one would ever know there wasn't any glass in the windows."

"It would be a great location," said Ruth. "But there must be other good ones, given a whole city to choose from."

"You could say that about any location, anywhere. And this one *is* a Bld Ste in the 15th with a view of the Eiffel Tower, just as it said in the map margin."

Ruth made a face. "We're going to have to look inside, aren't we?" she said.

I nodded, but I didn't move. I was discovering that faced with this large, impersonal, foreign building I was losing my nerve. "Except," I said, "that there's obviously no one here now, so I don't really know if we'd be justified in trespassing."

"Don't lose it now," said Ruth, "you're the one who's kept the faith all along. Accident prone, Jo. Remember what Godzilla said, Clair is accident prone."

In we went.

Although dusk hadn't quite happened outside, the rain clouds were creating a good imitation of it. Inside the high barrier of the hoardings it was well advanced. Once we'd stepped through a door-that-wasn't-there into a huge, empty room, out of sight of the street, the available light dimmed to a mere glimmer. And when we tiptoed cautiously through the room and out into what seemed to be a long corridor the other side, it all but vanished.

"Stand still," whispered Ruth, "until our eyes grow accustomed. There may be holes in the floors or anything."

"I can *feel* my pupils dilating," I said, "but I can't see any more than I could before."

"Should we call out?" whispered Ruth. "In case she's in here?"

"We could," I said, "but what if someone else is in here as well? Let's just creep around a bit and get the feel of the place. How much can you see now?"

"Nothing," said Ruth.

"Likewise."

In fact, we could see slightly more than nothing. We could see enough to be sure that the shadowy corridor was empty, and each time we peered carefully into one of the rooms, we could tell that there was nothing at all on the floor, nothing against any of the walls – nothing hanging from the ceiling, not even a light fitting.

"I wish we had a torch," I said, "this is really getting on my nerves."

"I've just remembered," said Ruth suddenly, scrabbling in her bag, "I have got one. On my key-ring."

The keys rattled as she pulled it out and we both grabbed them at the same time to hold them still.

"What if there *is* a dog?" said Ruth. "Or dogs? What do we do if one suddenly comes at us? Should we have a plan?"

"There can't be any," I said, hoping I sounded more confident than I felt, "they'd have heard us by now, they'd be barking or growling."

I took the torch from her and turned it on and we began to shudder our way along the long central corridor, glancing into a seemingly endless supply of weirdly empty rooms as we passed.

"This torch must have the smallest beam in the universe," I said. "I can't see the floor, I can't even see the floorboards, it just highlights individual splinters."

"It's only meant to light up a keyhole," said Ruth. "At home I have a great torch, a real dazzler, but I didn't bring it. I should have guessed a day trip to Paris would involve creeping around a derelict building in the dark, but I didn't. How crazy can you get."

That was when we heard it for the first time.

Neither of us knew what it was, but both of us

pinned ourselves back against the corridor wall and clutched each other.

We waited for long, long seconds, in total shivering silence, listening. All we could hear, though, was distant traffic outside the building.

I put my mouth right up to Ruth's ear and whispered, "What was it?"

In a whisper so soft I could hardly hear it, Ruth said, "I think it was a growl. For the first time today, I wish the twins were here."

"Whatever for?"

"Because then I could throw them to the dogs while I run for it."

"Ruth Riley!" I whispered, not so quietly as before because by now I'd decided we'd imagined the sound in the first place. "I'm shocked. You don't behave well under pressure."

The sound came again and we both froze. It still sounded something like a growl, but this time we both thought it was more human than doglike.

"Let's get out of here," said Ruth.

"It's a long way off," I said, "and it wasn't any closer the second time. Can you make out where it came from?"

"Ahead," said Ruth. "Look down the end there, at the left – is that a staircase going up, do you think?"

"Yes, it must be."

"I think it came from there. But if you think I'm going up to see what's at the top of the stairs you can forget it. Anyway, I've just realised what it is."

"What?"

"A wino or some other kind of derelict. Anyone

could get in here, and if it wasn't a large dog, then it was definitely a man – not a woman."

"Ruth," I said, grabbing her arm and shaking it, "what if we were right at the beginning and she *is* smuggling drugs and Godzilla and Jean Deguand *are* trying to hijack them and they've kidnapped her and they're holding her here for ransom – or something?"

"You're out of your head," whispered Ruth. "That doesn't even make sense. If those two *are* bad guys, they've got the camera case anyway, why would they capture her?"

"It would explain why she disappeared."

"Maybe, but that's about all it *would* explain. And that voice, if it was a voice, was *not* a woman's voice."

"Maybe she's been cornered by a wino who's growling at her!"

"Get real," said Ruth. Then, after thinking about it for a few seconds, she changed her mind. "I suppose that's possible," she said. "Okay, well what we do is get out of here right now and call the cops."

She turned back the way we'd come – but, to my surprise, I found myself sidling on alone, sliding my back along the corridor wall and then pushing my feet forward to keep up with it. I was scared, and I knew it would be far more sensible to leave with Ruth, but curiosity was too strong. I'll just have a quick look and then run, I was saying to myself in my mind, just a quick look, a very quick look.

Ruth said later that she'd got most of the way to the exit before she realised I wasn't with her and came back for me. By then I was nearly at the stairs.

Just before the stairs, though, on the left, I noticed that part of the wall seemed blacker than the rest. I turned the torch beam onto it. Feeble though the light was, it should have been able to make a glow on a wall that was only a few inches away. But it didn't. It shone through where the wall should have been and then gave up and stopped. I don't mean the torch went out, I mean the weak beam just faltered in mid-air and faded into nothing, unable to reach anything solid on the other side of the darkness.

The sound came again.

It wasn't a growl, it was a groan, and it came from way below my feet. I pointed the torch downwards and its faint light seemed to suggest a floor way below with something lumpy on it.

Ruth, realising I wasn't with her and thinking someone had grabbed me, came back at a run. I put out my arm to stop her.

"Careful," I said, speaking at normal volume for the first time since we'd come in. "It's a lift shaft – and I think someone's fallen down it."

"Is there anybody there?" came a man's voice, from deep within the shaft. "Oh thank God – if I have to sing myself one more chorus of *Scotland the Brave* I shall go completely out of my head."

CHAPTER FIFTEEN

An Unusual Angle

The man talking out of the dark pit didn't sound drunk, drugged, deranged or dangerous – just desperate.

"Are you badly hurt?" I called into the darkness.

"Not too bad, I don't think. Rotten twisted ankle, and I can't see to check the camera gear, but the real problem is there's no way of climbing up out of this. Will you be getting help?"

"Of course," I said. "At once. Do you want one of us to stay with you till it arrives?"

"You're all right," said the voice. "I'm getting used to my own company."

"How did it happen?" said Ruth. "What are you doing in here?"

"Looking for an unusual angle," said the voice. "I didn't want anything *this* unusual, though. I'm a photographer, believe it or not. An entire fashion shoot team must be cursing my name. They had all the locations set up and then I had to try and be clever and come up with something new, didn't I."

"I'm confused," I said, "we're looking for a fashion photographer who's gone missing. Clair Aitken."

"'That's me," said the voice. "I wondered what you were doing here. Are you part of the crew? I don't recognise your voices."

"*You're* Clair Aitken?" said Ruth.

"Ah," said the voice, "you were expecting a woman. It happens all the time. Clair's short for Sinclair – quite a common abbreviation in Scotland. I'm sorry I've caused so much bother – I've always been a wee bit accident prone, but I've never done anything quite this daft before."

Despite what he'd said, we couldn't really leave him alone like that, so Ruth stayed while I and my limited French ran to get help.

When we discussed the day-trip later, we realised the only time either of us set foot inside a French restaurant was when I went to the one round the corner to ask the manager to call the emergency services.

Then I went back to the building site and Ruth and I crouched on the floor by the lift shaft. We shone the dim torch to give him something to focus on, and we dropped my remaining peppermints down by way of comfort.

"Darkness isn't all bad!" he said. "If I could see how dirty these things are by the time I find them on the floor, I probably wouldn't be able to eat them."

He seemed remarkably cheerful – didn't really complain at all – just said he felt as though that particular Tuesday had been entirely ripped out of the calendar of his life.

To make up for it, we filled him in on how we'd

spent it. Except we missed out the bit about having to work so hard to get over to Paris in the first place.

We told him about Jean Deguand – ("Oh yes, the Frenchman on the plane.")

We told him about Bob – ("The shoot designer, known as the Yeti. Glad he's got the case safely.")

We also told him about the power women – though we didn't let on that the tour wasn't a genuine one. You can't give away all your secrets, even to an invisible man trapped in a pit.

In return, he told us that he'd always known Quest was a reliable firm, but he had no idea it extended its customer-care quite so far. "What service!"

He told us he always shredded paper when he found himself inside an extremely heavy metal contraption which, by some sort of unbelievable magic, had got itself three thousand feet up into the air.

He told us how the team had tried to get permission in advance to do some shots in this building. Then they discovered that the company working on it had gone broke, and had given up. Not wanting to let go of a good idea, Clair had decided to have a quick look on the way in from the airport, in the hope they might be able to use it anyway.

He added that Marco was a new model, one they'd never used before, "And now he's let us down, we won't use him again. It's crucial to be reliable in this game."

"Well, you'd know all about that," said Ruth, rather unkindly I thought, but just then the emergency services arrived, and his answer was lost in all the general hoo-hah of heaving him out and checking him over.

The extraordinary thing was that we never actually saw him. He came up out of the darkness hidden by a wall of police and paramedics, and Ruth and I – not entirely sure how the French felt about trespassing, even in a good cause – managed to slip away unnoticed.

It was a good thing we did because we'd lost so much time rescuing him that we realised we either had to get a cab to the airport or miss the plane. We chose the cab. "We can afford it," said Ruth resignedly, "it's not as if we spent all our money on meals or anything."

As we bounced and rattled our way out to Roissy, behind a short, angry-looking driver who didn't speak once, Ruth said, "Suppose you got the chance of a date with any one of the men we've met today, which would you pick? Jean, Tom, Bob or Clair?"

"Sinclair," I said, "definitely."

"You're very formal all of a sudden."

"I get confused if I try to think of him as Clair."

"I thought you'd say Tom," said Ruth. "Why Clair? Sinclair, sorry."

"Because he's a mystery man," I said. "He doesn't seem quite real – it's easier to fantasise if they're not quite real. He had a nice voice, didn't you think?"

"Aha," said Ruth, "you *are* interested. Okay, here's the story. He tracks us down through Quest and says he wants us – no, he wants *you* – to model for him in his next assignment. How's that?"

"Unlikely," I said. "*He* didn't see *us*, either."

"I think that could be an advantage," said Ruth.

I looked down at myself, then at her. I saw what she meant. We hadn't exactly been dressed to impress to start with. Now, what with being rained on, and spending time grovelling around a grubby building site, we looked indescribable. I wondered if that was why the cab driver was so bad-tempered. Possibly he was concerned for his upholstery.

"Clair can be your fantasy," said Ruth, "but don't wimp out on reality."

I said I didn't know what she meant.

"You do, too," said Ruth. "And stop pointing at the back of the cab driver's head. He doesn't understand a word I'm saying, and even if he did it wouldn't matter because he doesn't know you. But I know you! Clair really might come in to the Quest shop to say thanks and if something comes of it, that's fine – but don't you dare hide behind the brochure racks if Tom turns up."

"There are two myths about me," I said, "one is that I lose things and one is that I'm frightened of men. They are not true. Myths never are."

"Myths have their own truth," said Ruth. "If someone like Tom was going to call me I'd be looping the loop without a plane."

"Why are you so impressed by Tom all of a sudden? You were very scornful at first – you called him The Beach Boy."

"I changed my mind," said Ruth, "after a closer look. And *your* eyes lit up the moment he swung into view."

"I'm tired," I said, "and I don't think he will call. And I don't want to think about it, all right, because I don't want to be disappointed, fair enough?"

"Fair enough, I guess," said Ruth, with a sigh.

After all that, just two more things happened; one

that wasn't surprising at all, and one that definitely was.

The unsurprising thing was that we collapsed into our plane seats and slept solidly through the skies to London, missing out on our second chance of airline food, and not really improving our appearances.

The surprising one was that as we stumbled, dazed, through customs and immigration and out into the main part of the terminal building, we saw that someone had come to meet us. Bill. He was standing back from the crowd, watching. He saw us at once and came over.

"What are *you* doing here?" I said, amazed.

"Just gave a stewardess friend a lift down here," said Bill "so I thought I'd stick around and see if you two would like a ride home."

He looked us up and down. This time he looked at both of us, me too, not just Ruth. Then he raised one eyebrow to match his lopsided smile. "I see you managed to resist the temptation to buy clothes," he said.

"I realise I don't look exactly chic," I said snappishly.

"Chic is not the first word that springs to mind when I look at either of you," said Bill. "Mind you, I'm not quite sure that one word would be enough. If you asked me to be honest I'd have to say you look like something the cat wouldn't have had the heart to drag in."

"We didn't ask you to be honest," snarled Ruth.

"Never mind," said Bill, cheerfully. "I'll be helpful instead and take you kids home to your eagerly waiting parents."

He led us through the crowds to the short-stay car park and unlocked the door with a flourish of the electronic key.

"What on earth have you been up to?" he said as we got in. "I picked up one of the downstairs phones in passing and got a real earful from some Australian woman – client of yours, apparently. Then a bit later on your father got a long, incoherent speech of gratitude from some Scotsman calling himself Clair."

"It's a long story," said Ruth, "but it doesn't have any food in it."

That was how we ended up in a late-night Thai restaurant with Bill, eating prawns with ginger and mounds of rice and stir-fried vegetables, telling him the tale as slowly as possible to keep up the suspense.

"Well, it worked for the Australians," said Bill. "They were burbling with praise. Said they'd been taken down the kind of streets guides don't usually bother with."

"We thought they were going to ring and complain," said Ruth.

"Far from it," said Bill.

"They may have had a good time," I said, suddenly depressed, "but I don't think Ruth did."

"Me?" said Ruth. "I had the best time. Other people's day trips are so predictable."

"It was stupid, though," I said, "to take someone else's case through for them. There could have been all sorts in it."

"Hardly," said Bill, "not after your mother and I went through it with a fine-toothed comb." He looked up from peeling a prawn. "You knew she'd checked it, didn't you?" he said.

"Of course she did," said Ruth, before I could open my mouth, "she just thinks she should have checked it out herself as well."

"That would have been overkill," said Bill, going back to his prawn. "No, you're a good kid, Jo, you've done well."

"It was mostly bluff," I said, deciding to be honest.

"An ability to bluff is one of the essential skills," said Bill. "Anyone who can bluff an entire tour *and* manage to save a client's life on the side must have some kind of future in the travel business."

"You mean he might have died?" said Ruth. I don't think either of us had thought of that.

"He wouldn't have stayed healthy for ever," said Bill. "Your father's a happy man, Jo. Especially as you seem to have made him money. Your Mrs Cooper and Mrs Mackenzie are recommending Quest European Tours to all their rich Australian friends. *And* they want to book themselves on to some similar city tours as soon as possible. They're extending their stay in Europe specially."

"Good grief," said Ruth, "I don't know if we could make it work twice!"

"You won't get the chance," said Bill. "This time we employ grown-ups."

"Thanks for the vote of confidence," said Ruth.

"Oh, you'll make it one day," said Bill. "Both of you. You're born highflyers."

"Maybe – but there's never going to be another day like today," said Ruth.

"Stick around," I said, "I may decide to use my initiative again before long."